"I've made a terrible mistake."

Carin frowned, a puzzled expression on her delicate brow. "What mistake?"

"I apologized for what happened at the canyon this morning."

She shook her head. "I don't—"

David sat up and reached out to her, taking her onto his lap. "I should never have apologized for doing what I've wanted to do ever since you walked into that boathouse."

She smiled suddenly, a radiant expression that went right to his heart. "Then I won't accept the apology."

He tried to smile, but when she leaned down to touch her lips to his, the expression faltered. It didn't matter that she was as different from him as night from day, or if he said something was white, she'd say it was black. As his tongue tasted her, as his hands pushed aside the towel she was wearing, he had the shattering knowledge that she was becoming part of his soul.

ABOUT THE AUTHOR

Mary Anne Wilson is the author of a dozen romances
seasoned with adventure and suspense. She has made
Waldenbooks's bestseller list, was a Rita finalist and has
been a two-time Reviewer's Choice Nominee for the
Romance Writers of America. A true romantic, she
married her first love and lives with him in Southern
California with their three grown children and an odd
assortment of dysfunctional pets. This is her first book
for Harlequin.

MARY ANNE WILSON

HART'S OBSESSION

Harlequin Books

TORONTO • NEW YORK • LONDON
AMSTERDAM • PARIS • SYDNEY • HAMBURG
STOCKHOLM • ATHENS • TOKYO • MILAN
MADRID • WARSAW • BUDAPEST • AUCKLAND

To Maureen Walters and Susan James
—a great team

Published July 1993

ISBN 0-373-16495-5

HART'S OBSESSION

Prologue

The impact jolted him out of one world and into another. The sound of terror filled the air, a gut-wrenching shearing noise that tore at his soul. Then a scream, high and keening, a flashing brilliance, followed in the next heartbeat by a crushing blow to his chest that robbed him of all air.

David Hart was hurled forward, light and dark flashing past him. But before he could comprehend the images and sounds, he struck something hard and unforgiving, and his pain took on a life of its own. It caught every cell of his being, searing from his head to his shoulders, down into his arms and pummeling his body and legs.

For a fleeting moment, David inhaled something pungent and harsh, then he plunged into a world of blackness. The only thing he understood was the pain. As it built, as it grew to a crescendo of misery, he sank into a place that held a terror that had no name.

Time was gone. Life was drifting away, and David knew everything was over. No life flashing past his eyes, no regrets, no questions, just a knowledge that whatever happened, he couldn't stop it.

But as that simple acceptance came, he felt a linking with someone. He couldn't see anything, but there were hands on him. Holding him. Touching. Voices he couldn't understand. Movement. Being lifted. And the pain was there again, a pain that had no words to define it. He was suffocating, unable to take any air in, then as suddenly as everything started, it stopped.

There was nothing.

Chapter One

David bolted up to a sitting position, his hands braced at his sides and his heart beating so violently in his chest that it made him feel nauseated. Darkness and shadows were everywhere, the world undefined and blurred, and the only sounds were his own ragged breathing and the hammering of his heart in his chest.

At first, he had no idea where he was, what time it was, or what he was doing. Then as he inhaled the scent of earth and canvas, finally heard the chorus of insects and night birds on the night air, and felt the sultry air brush his bare skin, he knew where he was. Mexico. On the archaeological site. In his tent at the far side of the dig. His hand gripped the wooden frame of the cot where he'd been sleeping. Reality.

He shifted, pressing his feet to the coolness of the packed earth floor in the twelve-by-twelve-foot tent, and sat forward. With his elbows on his knees, he rested his head in his hands. As his heart began to beat at a more normal rate, he exhaled in a rush. Dammit, he never dreamed. Never. Not since he'd been a little kid and Daniel had told him outlandish stories about ghosts and monsters.

He rubbed his face roughly with both hands, his skin damp and clammy. As he dropped his hands to his thighs, he looked around the tent. In the semidarkness, he could make out the blur of shapes, the stack of boxes with his notes for the dig. Suitcases were pushed into the corner by the open flap. Nightmares. No monsters. No ghosts. Just a bad mixture of feeling drained after dealing day in and day out with inquisitive students who were like human sponges and the weariness that always came when he neared the end of fieldwork.

As a night bird screeched in the distance, he reached for the bottled water he'd left on a box by his cot, drank down almost half of it, then put it back. Ghosts and monsters were Daniel's domain, not his. The world of fantasy that his twin lived in when he wrote his novels was a world that David had no part in and never understood. Nor did he want to.

He settled back on the cot, stretched his six-foot frame on the canvas support and stared at the ceiling. Identical twins, yet Daniel lived a life so far removed from his that any resemblance ended after the physical. Daniel wrote novels, all about a private detective called T. J. Pierce, a rogue investigator. He spent most of his time in a fantasy world. On the flip side, David was a professor of archaeology who dealt in fact, in solid reality.

"God, that's boring," Daniel had said more than once.

David loved defending his chosen field. Archaeology fascinated him. It made sense to him. And he was as caught up in it as Daniel was in his novels.

"Hell, I don't call myself King Tut," David had countered. "Like you call yourself T. J. Pierce."

"T.J. lives because of me and through me," Daniel had said with a grin on his face, but a ring of truth in his words. "I created him. He's all mine."

Daniel had always blurred the lines between reality and fantasy, even when they'd been children. That was who Daniel was. Daniel. He usually saw his brother three or four times in a year, whenever they could work it out in their schedules. But now David realized they hadn't seen each other since last Christmas.

He rested his hands on his stomach and closed his eyes, thankful that all the images were gone. In three days the session would end and he could head to Berkeley to get ready for the fall semester. And on the way, he'd stop in San Diego to see Daniel. He had a couple of weeks before he had to get back to work. And he was heading that way anyway.

As sleep nudged him, he found himself almost testing it, to see if it held any more horrors. But as he sank deeper and deeper into it, he knew the nightmare was gone.

THREE DAYS LATER, David arrived at the marina where Daniel's houseboat was anchored. The taxi let him off by the entry, and with the tote bag he was carrying, he headed toward the docking area. As he stepped onto the floating dock, the sun was sinking low in the west and starting to spread the tint of twilight on the calm waters.

As he passed millions of dollars' worth of yachts, catamarans, sailboats and houseboats, he inhaled the saltiness of the balmy air. He saw seabirds swooping low over the dark waters, catching pieces of bread that an elderly lady was tossing to them from a sixty-foot schooner called *Merl's Delight.*

When she spotted David, she lifted a hand in greeting, then turned back to the birds who were settling on the water, waiting for more food. David knew she probably thought he was Daniel. When people looked at the two of them, they saw mirror images: lanky men, just over six feet tall, both with brown hair streaked with gray, deep-set hazel eyes and strong, solid features.

From a distance she couldn't notice that his hair was shorter than Daniel's, that he wasn't wearing jeans and a T-shirt—Daniel's favorite clothes—or that he was clean shaven instead of sporting the scruffy beginnings of a beard.

He looked ahead and spotted Daniel's houseboat, the fifty-foot vessel a colorful spot in an area of dark water and other boats done mostly in whites, natural wood and canvas. Daniel had his boat painted white, with red and blue stripes circling the hull and every piece of trim done in the same colors.

"I'm no damned patriot," Daniel had often said with a grin when David said something about the red, white and blue color scheme. "Just love those primary colors. They spice up life, get my blood flowing and my imagination running wild."

As if Daniel needs the stimulus David thought as he strode down the short ramp and stepped onto the deck near the entrance door. As he looked around, he knew Daniel wasn't here. There were no sounds of music from inside and the curtains were all closed. Daniel didn't go more than two minutes without the beat of rock music on the stereo, and the curtains were never closed when he was inside. Something about blotting out the sun. He hated it.

He knocked on the door once, then tried the brass knob. When it didn't give, he took out his keys, found Daniel's and opened the door. As he stepped into the dimness, he knew he'd been right. Daniel wasn't here. He glanced around the space of the combined living and sleeping area—the low ceiling above, wooden floors with red throw rugs underfoot, and the bed in the middle of the room with a royal blue spread and red throw pillows.

White wicker chairs and a matching couch with red and white striped cushions had been grouped near the draped doors that gave access to the viewing deck. A work area ran the full length of the opposite wall and was painted in those ever-present primary colors.

David swung the door shut, then crossed to the bed and dropped his bag on the floor. "Daniel!" he called, but his voice echoed back to him in the emptiness.

He sank down on the side of the bed and felt weariness tug at him. A lingering hangover made his head vaguely fuzzy. Parties on the last night of a dig were a tradition, but he'd been particularly untraditional last night by almost finishing off a bottle of tequila single-handedly. He'd been paying for it ever since. The headache was almost gone, and the dryness in his mouth was bearable.

He ran a hand over his face. He had no idea where Daniel was or when he'd be back. Until his brother showed up, he'd just have to wait. He unbuttoned his shirt, slipped it off and laid it across the footboard of the bed, then stepped out of his shoes and socks.

With a sigh, he sank back on the bed and stretched out. He'd wait. If Daniel didn't show up in a few days, he'd head home. He closed his eyes, and with the slight movement of the boat under him, he drifted off to sleep.

AS HE SLEPT, he felt he was in a place of comfort, a deep, peaceful place. The next moment, he was thrown back into the nightmare, as if it had never stopped.

Images flashed around him and cut through him, and he knew a terror that had no words to describe it. A terror so complete and overwhelming that it had a life of its own.

It beat him and absorbed him and brought an assault of a raw pain that was all-encompassing. It possessed him, taking his breath. Screams echoed in his mind, screams that couldn't push their way past a throat clenched painfully shut.

"It's a dream, a nightmare," he told himself, yet as he recited sanity, he felt the red fire of pain in his head, radiating down into his shoulders and back, until it circled his chest in an agonizing crush.

The pain went beyond anything he'd known before. When it became something that defied definition, when he couldn't endure any more, it stopped as suddenly as it had begun.

There was nothing. Nothing. Then slowly, he felt himself rising, drifting, going higher and higher, floating up into a darkness as soft as velvet and as inviting as peace. It shrouded him, cutting off the cold and sending the memory of the pain into a hidden place of forgetfulness.

Dying. He was dying. He knew it, yet it held no fear for him. It ceased to have meaning. In the dream he drifted up, up, up, until he could sense a glow beyond the darkness. A warmth that drew him and carried him upward with a promise to banish all his suffering. Forever.

"Go, just let go," he told himself. *"Let go."*

But before he could actually see the light, before he could reach out and find its brilliance, a jolt of fire shot through him. It seared into his soul, stopping him and wrenching him downward. Then another jolt came, followed by a third, and he plunged backward, hurling into the darkness. And in a single heartbeat, he was thrown out of the dream.

David sat up, a cold sweat sheening his skin. "A nightmare," he gasped, needing to hear that rational description said out loud in an effort to stop the nightmare's lingering effects.

A tingling stayed with him from the jolts that had rocked him. His breathing was tight and shallow. The darkness felt like a smothering cloak. Groping to his right on the table, he flicked the switch of a side lamp and a low light came on.

The glow made him blink a few times, then as his eyes focused, he knew with certainty that he was out of the nightmare. He was awake and sitting in the middle of the bed, the spread tangled around his legs.

With a harsh exhale he fell back in the mussed linen and closed his eyes. Why now? Why nightmares? He pinched the bridge of his nose between his thumb and forefinger as the headache began to resurface. He never dreamed. Intellectually, he knew it was humanly impossible not to dream, but as an adult, he had never remembered them, or pulled them into consciousness until the nightmare in Mexico.

He forced himself to breath evenly and deeply, to make his heartbeat slow until it almost matched the slight rhythm of the water rising and falling under the boat. That's what it had been, another nightmare. A product of too little sleep, too much bad food, too much muggy Mexican weather, and too much tequila last night.

He wasn't dead. Not even close. This was reality, not the nightmare. He was here, in one piece, on the houseboat.

He exhaled, then quickly opened his eyes when the clinging fragments of the nightmare nudged at him again. But as he stared at the ceiling, he couldn't shake the memory of floating out of his body, seeing the light, knowing he was dying, and almost letting go.

Dreaming about death in his brother's bed wasn't exactly the way he'd envisioned spending his free time. In frustration, he threw his hand to his side, hitting the bed with a thud. "Damn it, Daniel, where the hell are you?"

Right then, someone started banging on the entry door and David glanced at the clock radio by the bed. Just past eleven-thirty. Almost midnight, and one of Daniel's friends had decided to visit. He thought about waiting for the person to give up and go away. But the banging didn't stop.

With a muttered oath, David reached for his shirt and shrugged into it. Leaving it unbuttoned and un-tucked, he headed barefoot across the hardwood floor. As his headache intensified, he cursed the person who kept hammering on the door.

"Enough, enough," he yelled as he grabbed the cold brass knob and jerked back the wooden barrier. "What in the hell are . . . ?"

His voice trailed off when he saw a woman in the entry. She was backlit by the security lights from the dock, and all David could make out was her height, about five and a half feet, and a slender figure defined by dark pants and a clinging white blouse. The lights behind her made the tumble of pale hair that fell onto her shoulders look like a soft halo.

But before he could think strange things about halos and angels, she came toward him. As she adjusted the strap of her small shoulder bag, he inhaled freshness and delicate blossoms mingling in the air around him. He was looking into dark eyes shadowed by lush lashes, and a delicately boned face with a small straight nose and high cheekbones. She also possessed incredibly provocative, pale pink lips.

He was about to ask her what was going on, but before he could get out a word, she was speaking quickly in a low, slightly husky voice. "Thank goodness. You know I don't give up easily, but I was just about to leave. I thought that banging would wake the dead or at least your neighbors. If I hadn't seen the light, I wouldn't have knocked at all, but I've been trying and trying to contact you."

She brushed past David, and he jerked back when the silk of her blouse skimmed across his bare chest.

"You are the *hardest* person in the world to find. I know you told me you were horrible at keeping appointments, and I know we left it open, but I told you it was imperative that we talk before I headed out. I left messages and messages but you didn't get back to me."

She thought he was Daniel, just the way the lady had earlier. She went to the center of the room, then turned, still talking, and he wondered if she ever stopped to take a breath. "But it's important that we take care of things. It's not something that I can just let go, and you're going to... have to..."

Her rush of words slowed, then faltered and finally came to a stop. But it wasn't to take a breath. She was openly staring at David, then abruptly she went to the arched entry for the small kitchen and flipped a switch that turned on an overhead light. As brightness flooded the room, she moved back to the center of the room, and he could tell her eyes were a deep, almost navy blue. She frowned, and those darkly lashed eyes were studying him with such intensity that it was making him uneasy.

"What's going on here?" he asked.

But she didn't answer. She just kept staring.

He swung the door shut without looking away from her. "I don't know what you think you're doing, but—"

He braced himself when she slowly walked toward him, stopping a mere two feet from him. Her eyes widened, her lips parted, then she breathed. "David?"

Whatever he'd expected, it wasn't his name. God knew he'd never met her. She wasn't a woman any man would forget seeing, not matter how fleetingly.

"You're David, aren't you?" she murmured.

Her tongue darted out to touch her full bottom lip, and he held his breath when she took another step toward him. "Who are you?" he managed.

"Carin Walker." She took another step, effectively erasing most of the space between them. Her face was turned up. For one crazy moment, David thought she was close enough to kiss. That idea almost exploded in him when he realized he could feel the heat of her body through the thin cotton of his shirt. "And you're the infamous David. The archaeological professor brother, aren't you?"

He hated being taken off guard like this, and he hated the effect this stranger was having on him. He'd always believed instant attraction was invented by oversexed college kids. Another belief shattered. First, nightmares where they had never been before, now this woman who only had to look at him to make him think crazy things.

He backed up half a pace while he crossed his arms. If he narrowed his eyes a bit, it blurred her image enough to take the edge off his crazy response to her. "You seem to know *me,* so who are you and why are you here?" he asked in his best professorial voice.

"I obviously came to see your brother, Daniel."

"And he told you about me?"

"He's told me a lot. He's a born storyteller, isn't he?"

"He makes his living at it," he muttered.

"I know." She spoke quickly. "It was pretty exciting to meet the man who wrote the T. J. Pierce detective series. He's so talented. You must be really proud of him."

"I am," he said.

She glanced over her shoulder at the mussed bed, then back to David, a faint frown tugging at perfectly arched eyebrows. "Could you let Daniel know I'm here?"

"I could, if he was here. He's not."

"When are you expecting him?"

"I expected him to be here when I arrived, but he wasn't, and I don't have a clue when he'll show up."

"When you talked to him, didn't he say when he'd be back?"

"I haven't talked to him for almost two months. I've been in Mexico, and—"

"He told me you were on some archaeological thing with some students from the university, something about a second level of a city near a pyramid, or an underground city. I don't quite remember."

"You're close enough. But it's done, and I had a break before heading back north, so I came to see Daniel."

She cocked her head to one side, those navy eyes openly skimming over him from head to toe. Just when he was getting really uncomfortable, she spoke. "It never ceases to amaze me how they throw around the word 'identical' about twins. No two people are exactly alike, even if they start out from the same egg. Two halves of a whole, but each half has its own uniqueness."

"What are you—?"

"You don't really think you're that much like Daniel, do you? Same general features and build, the same coloring and nose. But that's where the similarities end, don't you think?"

"Actually, yes, but—"

"See," she said as if he'd made a perfect point for her. "It's a misconception. Identical doesn't mean identical, as in one and the same, alike in every way." Her eyes narrowed. "But I bet you two could really fool people when you were younger, before you went off in opposite directions in life."

David wondered just how close Daniel was to this woman to tell her about him and their past. "Opposite directions? What are—"

"You know, you go off to college and get your degree and settle into the academic world, being a professor of archaeology, and Daniel takes off on his bike, wanders around, then finally falls into the perfect career for him—writing. It all seems so different and quixotic, doesn't it? I mean, the two of you start out—"

"Whoa," he said, holding out a hand palm while he tried to figure out just when he lost total control of this encounter. "I don't know what Daniel told you, but—"

"He told me everything," she said, cutting him off to make an uncharacteristically concise statement.

He exhaled, then opened his mouth to say something, anything, to break off this crazy conversation. But before he could even draw in a breath, Carin came half a step closer and started talking again, her voice lower, almost as if she was making him part of a confidential discussion.

"Did you ever think that being a twin was something special, or did you see it as a burden? Daniel seems to think that you hated it, that you deliberately took off in your own direction to prove how different you were from him. But, isn't that just what he did, too? I mean, he's involved in fantasy, not the—"

"That's it," he said bluntly. "Enough of this. Daniel's doing what Daniel wants to do, and so am I. And I don't know why in hell I'm even talking to you about this. My brother isn't here, and it's getting late."

She was quiet for a long moment, then released a breath on a sigh. "I'm sorry. Really, I am. I just get so carried away sometimes."

She was coming to see Daniel near midnight, and David had no doubt she could get carried away. As he looked into those navy eyes, his annoyance softened. He admitted there was actually something appealing about the breathy way she spoke, that low, husky intensity in her words.

And physically... he tried to block the natural progression of his thoughts, and the fleeting idea that Daniel had really outdone himself this time if Carin was his new girlfriend.

"I don't mean to rush you, but do you want to leave a message?" he asked.

She shrugged, a fluttery movement of slender shoulders under the ivory silk of her blouse. "I don't know. I'm leaving town for a while, and I'm not exactly sure when I'll be back. Daniel knows all about it. He told me he was going to be back days ago, and he knew I needed to see him before I left. But, I guess he got sidetracked somewhere."

David knew Daniel got sidetracked very easily. "He probably did. Just where was he going?"

"To do research for his new book. He had a lot of facts he needed to check out, and he was going to travel through the southwest, Arizona and New Mexico, and be back in three weeks. That was a month ago. I haven't heard from him since he left."

"Daniel seldom checks in with anyone."

"I know that."

"If you know that, then you know he's not exactly a creature of habit."

"I know Daniel owns one clock, the one by his bed, and that he's never owned a wristwatch. It's just he gave me his word, and no matter how loose and fast he plays with timetables, I know his word means something."

She was dead-on target with that. "Just what did he promise you?" he asked, almost hating to find out.

"That he'd be back in three weeks, then we could spend some time together before I had to leave."

David had no idea why it was suddenly so distasteful to him that this woman was another in a string of women who flitted in and out of Daniel's life. "If you know Daniel so well, you'd better know that he's about as constant with a woman as earthquakes are forecastable."

She stared at him, eyes wide, then he could have sworn she blushed. Color brushed her cheeks. "Oh, no, you think... No, it's not like that with Daniel and me. I mean, we're not like that, not at all."

"You and Daniel aren't like what?" He knew he was watching the first woman he'd ever met who actually blushed. More color stained her delicate cheeks and even the tip of her nose. Where in the hell did Daniel ever find a woman who could blush? He saw her take a breath, then lift her chin a bit.

"You think Daniel and I are, you know, an item, don't you?"

"Aren't you?"

"No, not at all."

"You're just friends?"

"Yes, well . . . no, not really . . ."

"Miss Walker, I know my brother, and I know that he's not into platonic relationships. If *you* knew him, you'd know that he isn't the sort to settle down in any sense of the word. Do you know what it cost him to finally get a house, such as this is? To actually put his Harley in a garage? The idea of having someplace permanent scared him to death."

The color was lessening. "I know. He told me that being tied down was akin to being put in prison." She shook her head, stirring the soft curls on her shoulders, and ever so slowly, a wry smile tugged at her lips. "Believe me, I don't have any illusions about Daniel."

The instinct to back up, to put some distance between himself and a girlfriend of Daniel's who could blush, then smile in a way that made his breath catch, was overwhelming. "Then you're the first woman he's been involved with that didn't," he murmured.

The smile was gone, replaced by the frown that he realized came when she was studying him with those navy eyes. "You don't see Daniel too often, do you?"

"When I can."

"Which is . . . ?"

"Two or three times a year," he admitted.

She shook her head again, as if she didn't approve. "Strange. Most twins need more contact. Some twins can't live separately, or live very far from their other half."

"Miss Walker—"

"Carin," she said quickly as she kept talking. "Don't you find it fascinating how open Daniel is about himself? Usually people aren't very objective about themselves, but Daniel is, even about his own failings. He certainly doesn't hide from them." She came even closer, the frown intact. "He's incredibly intuitive—"

David wasn't about to stand here, barefoot, near midnight, listening to a beautiful blonde enumerate the attributes of his brother. Not when she smelled of freshness and flowers and a delicateness that radiated from her. "Why don't you tell me why you're here, and when I see Daniel I'll pass on the message."

She kept talking as if he hadn't said a thing. "You know, the familial similarities are so strong, the nose, the jaw, even the shoulders, yet the body movements are different. Yours are more...how would I say it...controlled. That's it. Controlled."

"What are you, an expert on twins or something?"

"I don't know about being an expert, but right now, twins *are* my work."

He felt a tension building at the base of his neck. "I'm sure I'll be sorry I asked, but what does that mean?"

"I'm a research psychologist."

"And?" he prodded, knowing all too well where this was going.

"I'm doing a study on the links between twins."

David rolled his eyes. Not a girlfriend, but a head doctor putting his brother under a microscope to see what made twins tick. "What sort of link?"

"Intangibles."

"Translate that to psychic?"

"If you want to call it that."

"What do you call it?"

"Extrasensory interaction."

"Hocus-pocus."

"No," she said. "It's not hocus-pocus. It's a verifiable link between human beings."

He knew he wasn't up to being studied by this lady's navy eyes, or for a discussion like this, especially not combined with the lingering uneasiness from the dream. "I don't know what Daniel agreed to do with you, but don't look at *me* like that. I don't want any part of it."

"Like what?" she said.

Tension was playing havoc with his neck muscles. "Like I'm a bug on a display board."

"I'm not. I don't do that."

"Oh, yes you do. You narrow your eyes and study me as intently as Einstein studied his equations."

"Mr. Hart," she said in a voice he was certain meant to smooth, "I'm sure you're just overreacting."

"Don't patronize me, *Dr.* Walker."

Color touched her cheeks again, but her voice stayed even. "I wasn't trying to. I'm just trying to figure out what's going on with you."

"Nothing's going on with me that isn't accounted for by you coming here in the middle of the night looking for Daniel, who's apparently disappeared."

Her eyes widened. "So, you think he's disappeared?"

He had no idea why he chose those words, yet even while he denied them, uneasiness slid up his spine. "I didn't mean disappeared, I meant that he's not here, he's not back."

"What if he has?"

"Has what?" he asked with exasperation.

"Disappeared? What if something's wrong?"

The uneasiness grew in strength until he crossed his arms on his chest again in an effort to distract himself. "Daniel's doing research," he said, pointing out what he considered perfect logic. "You said so yourself."

"And he was supposed to be back a week ago."

"So, he got distracted."

Her eyes narrowed, and he could feel her studying him again. "How do you know that?"

Carin stared at the man not more than five feet from her, the image of Daniel, yet a man so infinitely different from his twin that it only confirmed her own beliefs.

Despite her promise to David to stop scrutinizing him, she found herself doing that very thing. When she'd walked in, turned and realized he was David Hart, she'd been shocked and intrigued.

David would be the spitting image of his brother if Daniel had cut his hair shorter, shaved off his perpetual beard stubble, and if she'd ever seen him in twill slacks and an Oxford shirt instead of his usual jeans and T-shirt. Both men's features were strong, as if fashioned by a sweeping, sure stroke during creation, and they actually stood the same way, feet slightly apart, usually rocking forward on the balls of their feet.

Still, the difference was there, and she finally knew it was in the eyes. They shared the same shade of hazel, but their expressions were vastly different. Daniel had a perpetual look of ease, as if he was happy with his life and himself. On the other hand, David squinted when he got annoyed, or lifted one brow in question, and his mouth seemed tight, as if laughter didn't come easily.

Different, yet equal, she thought. Then another difference hit her. Daniel had an open, casual sexuality about him, whereas David had a more subtle sexuality. The term "slow burn" flitted through her mind before it was pushed out by an unsettling impression she was getting from David. It came from nowhere, and it shook her. She stared at him harder. Did David know something about his brother's absence?

Chapter Two

"I asked you not to do that," David said, cutting into her thoughts.

Carin had completely lost track of their conversation. "Excuse me?"

"You're looking at me as if I was a bug on display."

"I'm sorry. Really. I guess it's a bad habit." The apology was offhanded while her mind raced, wondering just how accurate Daniel's appraisal was of his twin. She'd dealt with twins before who had no connection, no special something between them. Or twins where one experienced it and the other didn't. "David's closed to anything like that, and totally into reality," Daniel had told her.

"Can I ask you something?" she said.

She didn't miss the heavy sigh that spoke of annoyance before David replied, "What is it?"

"In my research with your brother—"

"Just what exactly is your research?"

"I've been working with twins and involved in extrasensory connections."

"How exactly?"

"Through interviews, observation, some testing and some tracing of lineage."

He nodded, but didn't comment. She couldn't tell from his expression just what he thought.

"Mr. Hart, during my time with Daniel, he told me he believed that he had a certain connection with you, a sort of psychic bonding. And I—"

He cut her off abruptly, and Carin could see the tension in him growing as he spoke. "He also believed in Santa Claus until he was twelve."

"And you didn't?" Another difference.

"No, I didn't. And before you ask, I don't believe in UFO's, little green men, or Elvis sightings."

His mouth tightened even more and something in her wanted to see how he would look if he laughed, or if he just smiled. She raised one eyebrow. "You mean to tell me Elvis isn't pumping gas in Alabama?"

She got her wish for a smile, a curling at the corners of his lips that exposed the suggestion of a dimple to the left of his mouth. Daniel's was on the right side. Mirror images. Fascinating. But in the next heartbeat, her scrutiny went beyond scientific analysis. There was a light in his eyes, a certain gentling of him that made her breath catch, an expression that was as startling as heat lightning on a hot summer night. And that reaction stopped her dead.

"I can promise you he's not hanging out at a McDonald's in Florida, either," he said.

She blinked rapidly, trying to absorb the shock and form a decent facsimile of a smile. But she could feel the tightness in her expression. Had she thought this man's sexuality was subtle and understated? Boy, had she been wrong. With that expression, and the way he was rocking forward on the balls of his feet, the man had a sexiness that almost took her breath away.

She'd never looked at a subject with anything more than intellectual curiosity. In that moment she had the stunning knowledge that this had the ability to complicate everything. And that couldn't happen. "Too bad," she murmured. "I sort of liked the idea of Elvis still hanging around... somewhere."

"The King is dead, and so are fairy tales."

"Ever the realist?" she asked in a tone that sounded flat even in her own ears.

The smile was gone completely, vanishing as if it had never been, and she found that she could breathe a bit easier now. "And Daniel's the dreamer. That's why I lecture to eager college students about ancient civilizations, and Daniel sells fantasy for a living."

She tried to refocus her thoughts, deliberately looking away from the strong forearms crossed on his chest and the way his shirt was parted, exposing the strength of his chest and the suggestion of dark hair. "And you don't think there's any credence in psychic links, or strong intuitive feelings?" she asked, feeling the beginning of heat touching her cheeks at thoughts she was having a hard time ignoring.

He exhaled in a rush. "It's just psychobabble."

She could feel the heat grow, and for the millionth time in her life, she cursed the fact that she had no control over her blushing. "It's not psychobabble. And what I meant was, when you used the word 'disappeared' I had the feeling it wasn't a slip of the tongue, or simply the wrong choice of words."

"Just what did you think it was?" he asked, his hazel eyes meeting her gaze with an unblinking stare, as if he was daring her to say what she thought.

That didn't stop her. "I thought you might have had some intuitive feeling about why Daniel isn't back."

"Sorry to disappoint you, but the best intuitive feeling I've ever had was a couple of minutes ago when I knew I shouldn't have opened the door."

Her face was flaming now, but she'd be damned if she'd back down. "You've never had an intuitive experience with your brother?"

He uncrossed his arms and pushed both hands in the pockets of his slacks. As he rocked toward her, he muttered through clenched teeth, "No, and I'm not going to take an inkblot test to find out why I've never had one. Now, if you're finished—"

"You're not worried about Daniel?"

He hesitated and she knew she'd hit a nerve. "Daniel can take care of himself," he said.

"No doubts at all?"

"Okay, I'll tell you what I believe. Daniel is late. Daniel doesn't own a watch. He's never bought a calendar in his life, and doesn't have patterns."

"Everyone has patterns in their life, Mr. Hart, even people who wouldn't think that they have patterns."

"Not Daniel."

"Yes, he does. Even though Daniel told me that when he does research, he goes with the flow, takes his Harley and absorbs life, he's got his own patterns."

"I've never seen any, except his desire to not have patterns."

"I can see that people might perceive him that way, even you, but he's got a pattern of meeting his deadlines with his publisher. He's not a bad businessman. And he said that he calls in every so often whenever he's gone to get his messages, sort of a need to keep in touch even if he's out roaming.''

"What's your point, Doctor?"

"I've left a lot of messages in the past week, and he hasn't answered one of them.''

"So?"

She looked right at him. "He's broken a pattern.''

"How do you know he didn't call, get his messages, and just didn't bother to answer them?"

She motioned to the answering machine near the computer. "The light on his machine is flashing like crazy."

Carin knew David wanted nothing more than to have her gone, but instead of showing her the door, he went past her to the answering machine. "Let's see if your messages are here," he said as he pressed the play button.

Then a computerized voice said, "You have ten messages."

Carin watched David as the messages began, the date stamps starting just over a week ago. There were a couple of messages from friends, then two from his publisher needing to see his revised proposal, three in a row from Carin, followed by a message from David. "Daniel, I've got a break before the fall semester, I'm coming to see you. I'll fly out tomorrow morning. See you when I get there." The date stamp was yesterday, five minutes to midnight.

And right after that message was one last message from Carin. "Daniel, where are you? I've got to leave and it's imperative that you at least call before I go.

You've got the number.'' The date stamp was two o'clock this afternoon.

"That was your last message,'' the computer voice said, then the machine clicked to a stop.

Carin never took her eyes off David. He had his back to her, his head bowed, as if staring at the machine would make it say what he wanted it to. Finally, he turned to Carin.

His eyes were narrowed, making his expression even more unreadable, yet she could see the muscle working in his jaw. "He never contacted you at all, not once?'' he asked.

"No.'' She turned from his gaze to glance around the room, a room that she'd been in several times. Yet it had never seemed as small as it did now. Something about David had diminished the space, as surely as his nearness was making her very aware of the mussed bed and the pair of well-worn loafers sitting beside a duffel bag.

As she looked over to the door, she spotted a wire basket where the mail was collected on the far side. The woven metal container was overflowing. She crossed, crouched down and took out the stack of envelopes and advertising fliers.

She sorted through the lot, from a small padded envelope on top, to bills, a lot of junk mail, and a couple of larger envelopes with his publisher's return address. She felt David coming up behind her. "What are you doing?''

Distracting myself from you, she wanted to say, but didn't. "Just looking,'' she said as she put the fliers back in the basket. Then she stopped when she looked closely at the padded envelope that had been on top of the pile. "What's this?" she asked.

David reached down, brushing her shoulder with his arm to pick up the envelope. Carin stood and turned, glancing at David, then looking down at the envelope. She read the address. In a back-slanted scrawl, it said, To: T. J. Pierce. The address was for the houseboat. The postmark was too blurred to make out the origin, but she could see the date. Three days ago.

She'd moved closer to David to make sure what she thought she'd seen on the address was true, and when she looked up at him, she could see a pulse that beat at the hollow of his throat. "T. J. Pierce?" she asked. "Why would anyone address something to a fictional character?"

"Maybe it's a fan who can't separate fact from fiction," he murmured.

"Maybe, but I thought Daniel told me he never gave out his home address, that all of his mail went through the publisher."

He stared at the envelope. "There's no return address."

"Aren't you curious?"

His hazel eyes were as unreadable as ever when they lifted to meet her gaze. "It's my brother's mail."

"Technically, it's mail for a person who doesn't exist, and besides, you're here and he's not." She killed the urge to take it from him and tear it open. "I don't think it would hurt to open it."

David didn't know if he was still reeling from the dream, or if the sense of something being wrong came from the reactions he was having to this woman. Or maybe the intensity that seemed a permanent part of her was filtering into him. But he found himself moving away from her to go to the desk. He looked around, picked up a ballpoint pen and worked the tip under the two staples that held the envelope shut.

He worked the lip up, then emptied the contents onto the desktop. A dog-eared spiral-bound notepad, about three inches by five inches, that had a piece of torn paper stapled to its cover, fell onto the clutter of the desk. David picked it up and read the note aloud.

Found this on the road looking the worse for wear. Didn't know if it's important, but found address inside along with name, so sending it back.

The writing was the same as on the front of the envelope, but there was no signature, not even a date.

David left the note stapled to the front and opened the notebook. On the inside of the cover, in Daniel's writing, was his home address, and under it, the name, T. J. Pierce. Below that, "Notes for *Obsession*." On the page facing the cover was a crude map of what looked like the southwest corner of the U.S.—California, Arizona and New Mexico. Scale was nonexistent and a series of Xs along a single line that cut through all three states were obviously places, but not named.

"It's Daniel's," he said as he turned the pages. He sensed Carin behind him, coming closer, then he felt her hair brush his bare arm as she looked down at the notebook.

"What's it for?"

He felt a shiver that could have come from the feathery caress of her hair on his skin, or the growing sense of something being wrong about Daniel's absence. "Notes from his research." He flipped the pages. "Everything he needs for his new book," he said, inordinately aware of the way a delicate perfume seemed to cling to her.

"He said he couldn't even read his own writing sometimes. I can see why," Carin breathed, so close he could feel the heat of her breath on his shoulder through the shirt.

He closed his eyes for a moment, needing to center himself, but finding that center escaping him. He moved away from Carin under the guise of turning the book at a better angle to catch the light. "His writing's about as bad as mine, but I can make it out."

He glanced back at Carin, and her frown was back full force as she studied him. "He could put all of his notes for a whole novel in that small book?"

"He kept most of his research in his head. He lived those books when he wrote them. I think he became T. J. Pierce, rebel detective, Harley riding, wild, but always on the side of right and honor." He closed the notepad. "He just put down key words in here, thoughts that he didn't want to forget. He hated details, but knew he had to watch them to give the books credibility."

"And he dropped it somewhere along the way so someone found it and sent it here."

"Three days ago."

"How important do you think this book is to him?"

"Very important."

"If he knows he lost it, don't you think he'd be here now hoping someone would find it and send it back?"

"Probably."

"Then why isn't he here?"

"If I knew that, I'd know where he is."

She moved toward him, and before he knew what she was doing, she touched him on the arm, her fingers light and warm. Yet an electric shock couldn't have taken him more off guard. He looked at her, her eyes wide and serious. "Do you think we should call the police?"

"What?"

"The police. If Daniel's missing..."

He drew away from her touch and closed the book. "We don't know that he's missing, and even if I thought he was, once the police know how he does things, they won't take it seriously."

She slanted him a look and nailed him with her words. "Do you?"

He exhaled, feeling decidedly as if someone, namely her, had painted him into a corner. "I don't know," he said honestly.

"Aren't you the least bit concerned?"

"I wouldn't have opened my brother's mail if I wasn't concerned. Of course I'm concerned."

"Then what are you going to do about it?"

She was looking at him as if she was really worried about Daniel's whereabouts. He knew she was, and the thought was distasteful. Daniel was her subject, maybe even the core subject of her study. No wonder she was so concerned if her study was in jeopardy. "I'll figure out something."

She gave a small, startled gasp that made David start. "I just had an idea. Your family, maybe he went to see someone in the family, like your mother?"

Boy was she off the mark. "I don't think he—"

"Maybe he just decided to go and see her?"

"And maybe he didn't."

"Why wouldn't he?"

"Didn't Daniel tell you about our mother?"

"He said that your father died when you were both seven, and she remarried. I think he said she was living in New York."

"What he neglected to tell you is she's remarried four times, and that she was living in New York with some guy she said was a count, but he was in exile so he couldn't claim his birthright. Then she met an English earl, and as far as I know, she's divorcing the poor count and going for a British title. The last I heard, she was thinking of relocating to England with this guy."

She frowned, her head tipped to one side. "Daniel never told me any of that. He just said that your father died, that your mother remarried and you two weren't particularly close to her."

"Daniel's version of life is different from reality at times. I'm not surprised he didn't tell you all of that."

"Actually, I never got around to asking him about that. We spent most of our time talking about the thrust of the study, the idea of twins and their connections."

"It's obvious you were more interested in him being a twin than in him being a person."

Her face flamed, a disconcerting habit of hers that touched him in the most unexpected way. "All right, all right. Why don't we just clear the air and you tell me exactly what you have against what I'm doing with Daniel.''

He narrowed his eyes, trying again to take the edge off her image. ''It's hocus-pocus,'' he said bluntly. ''Did Daniel tell you about the so-called study we were put through when we were young?''

''He told me about your mother getting you involved in a study on twin development. You were about eight or nine when it started.''

''Did he also tell you that the one doing the study was Mother's second husband, a so-called behavioral scientist?''

''No, he didn't say—''

''That husband lasted eleven months. Did he tell you that he played games with the man, that he lied to him all the time, making up fantastic stories? That he did it to drive him crazy? The man took copious notes and spouted ideas about writing it up for some journal.''

''What was his name?''

That stopped him. He barely remembered the man. ''Basil something or other. Why?''

''If he wrote it up—''

''He never did anything. The divorce came so quickly, I'm sure the poor guy had other things to think about by then.''

''Daniel didn't tell me about the man being your stepfather, but he told me about the rest.''

''And you think he's been telling *you* the truth?''

''He's doing this study with honesty. But you're just about the same as you were then, aren't you?''

''What are you talking about?''

"Daniel said you wouldn't even talk to the man, that you refused to do the tests, and you wouldn't make up stories or play the game."

Once David found Daniel he was going to make sure he left him out of his sessions with the good doctor. He wasn't going to be dissected by a woman like this. "Oh, did he?"

"Was that the truth?"

"I don't play games."

"And I guess you haven't changed, have you?"

"No, I don't think I have. There's enough truth in this world to last for everyone's lifetime. We don't need screwball fanatics."

The color flared in her cheeks, but he could see real anger in her eyes. "I'm a screwball fanatic?"

"I never said—"

"And your *brother* was open enough to new ideas that he realized that this new research wasn't some voodoo exercise."

"And I'm close-minded?"

The color rose in her face again, but David found he was beginning to respect the fact that Carin wasn't the sort of woman to back down. "Are you?"

"I'm a realist, Dr. Walker. I don't live in some never-never world like Peter Pan."

"Land."

"What?"

"Never-never land, Mr. Hart, not never-never world."

"Is that where you're coming from?"

"I'm just a doctor who's trying to find a way to help figure out the mysteries behind the human condition, to get answers for unanswerable questions, to make life clearer, to help other doctors have a more solid foundation for their therapies, to explore other ways of reaching out to each other." Her words rushed at him, words filled with defensiveness and real passion.

"Haven't you heard about twins who feel each other's pain, or twins who were separated at birth and when they finally meet, they not only look the same, but have the same occupation, comb their hair the same way, named their children the same names? Or when one twin dies and the other one dies minutes later for no reason?"

"I get the point," he said quickly, before she could keep going. The mention of death brought back the dream with a strength that shook him, almost as much as this woman's presence threw him off balance. "I've heard all of that before, many times. Now, if I can get a word in edgewise, can I make a point?"

She nodded as she crossed her arms on her breasts, all but shouting her closed-mindedness with her body language, but not saying a word.

"Doctor Walker, people are more than some scientific experiment. Life is a series of absolutes, causes and effects. It isn't some mystical condition where beings communicate by telepathy and exist only for each other."

He knew she wouldn't stay silent. "Obviously, you don't believe in anything that can't be seen, touched, tasted, heard or proven by a mathematical equation, do you?"

"No, I don't."

"You've never even considered the idea that when a single egg divides into two lives, that those lives are joined forever?"

"I've considered a lot of things," he said, wondering how any woman who was obviously as intelligent as she was beautiful, could be wrapped up in that nonsense. "Among them, the question of why people want to crawl into other people's heads and see what makes them tick."

Her eyes widened. "I get it. That's what you hated all the time, wasn't it?"

"What are you talking about now?" he asked with exasperation.

"It wasn't your mother having weird husbands, or Daniel being lost in fantasy, it was anyone getting too close to you, anyone getting to know the real you."

He wasn't going to do this, not now, not here and definitely not with her. "You don't have any right to analyze me. I'm not one of your subjects."

"Okay, okay," she said quickly. "I admit I get carried away, and I can see this is going nowhere, so why don't we agree to disagree?"

David was taken aback by the unexpected olive branch. He'd been certain she'd push this to the limit. "No more analyzing?"

"I'll try to control myself."

"Good."

"Now," she said. "Why don't we get started on deciphering his book?"

She reached for the notebook, her fingers closing over his that gripped the book, but David didn't let it go. "Just a minute," he said, ignoring the feeling of her slender hand on his. "Daniel's my brother, and whatever's going on, I'll take care of it."

"I want to help," she said, not drawing back either.

"He's my brother, and he's my problem."

"He's my..."

"Your what?" he asked.

Her lashes partially shaded her eyes, but he could see that moment of hesitation. "He's my friend," she finally said.

He broke their contact by pulling the book back and away from her. "Be honest, Doctor. He's your case study, your guinea pig. He's probably Subject X in your notes."

She drew her hand back to press it to her middle. "You really don't think I could care about him as a human being?"

"Do you?"

"Of course."

"Isn't that violating the rules of an impartial study, getting emotionally involved with a subject?"

"I'm not emotionally involved *that* way," she said, backing up a step.

"Then why are you here? Is it because you were really worried about Daniel, or is it to make sure that your prime subject isn't going to foul up your expensive study?"

"Daniel didn't tell me you were *this* cynical."

"I'm not cynical. I told you, I'm realistic. I've been through tests and studies of all kinds. I know how they work, and I know the kind of people who do them. And I know the way that some of those people can reach for the absurd to justify the expensive grant they are no doubt drawing money from." Her color deepened again and he pressed his point. "I'd lay odds you have a huge grant from someone who believes in fairy tales and you have to answer to him, her or them."

"None of that's your business," she countered, her chin lifting just a bit.

"You don't have masses of money behind you?"

"I've got enough."

"How much?"

"I told you that's none of your business, and as far as what you think of me, don't. You don't even know me."

He knew he was right. But she was right, too. All he knew was what she'd told him and what he could see of her. And that was enough to make him wish she was an ugly spinster in gray clothes and sensible shoes so he could think clearly and focus. "All right. Just give me one good reason why you're here if you're not here to protect your study results?"

Her tongue darted out to touch her pale lips, then she seemed to stand straighter. "I'm here to find out what happened to Daniel. I don't care what you think about my motives." She glanced at the book at his side, then slanted a look back at David. "What difference do my motives make if I can help you?" He heard the challenge in her words, and when she spoke again, he knew she'd neatly backed him into a corner...again. "Do you want to keep to your bias or do you want help finding your brother?"

"I want to find out what's going on with Daniel."

"And I really could help you. I nearly married a private detective."

He stared at her. "You nearly what?"

"A few years ago, I was engaged to a private detective. Hank always said that I had a sharp mind in analytical situations."

A fiancé? He didn't know why that thought took him so off balance. A woman who looked like Carin Walker certainly wouldn't go through this life without many men looking at her more than once. He was as good an example of that as anyone. But it had never even occurred to him that she could be engaged or maybe even married. "This Hank—"

"My ex-fiancé. I called it off over a year ago. I only brought it up because he was a private detective, and he said I actually had a very analytical mind. Now, Daniel talked to me about this trip because he knew that I'd been that way a lot of times. I know that he was going to head out on Interstate 8 into Arizona, then keep going east. I know that he asked about particular things, about types of land, towns along the way. I even recommended restaurants for him to stop at." She took a deep breath. "See, I wasn't planning to look into a crystal ball or put you under hypnosis to find Daniel. Now, can I help?"

Chapter Three

When Carin took a breath and would have started her argument again, David acted on impulse and reached out for her. Before he understood his own actions, he had her chin cupped in his free hand. "Please, let me get a word in edgewise," he breathed, knowing then what a mistake it was to make physical contact with this woman.

Silk would have been too rough a word for her skin, and when her lips parted in shock, he knew that midnight was the wrong time to have this woman this close to him and this close to the bed.

"All right," she whispered, and he drew back.

Even worse for David was he couldn't think of one rational-sounding reason to ask Carin to leave him alone to gather what sanity he could, except to tell her that she disturbed him. But that wasn't even an option. God knew what she'd do with that bit of information. "All we have is his book, and *I* can read that."

"But *I'd* know what to look for."

Perfect logic from a woman he'd begun to doubt knew the meaning of the word, he thought and unconsciously rubbed his hand on the rough twill on his thigh. "You've got a point. I planned on staying here for a while, so we might as well go through it, and see if it can tell us anything."

"Great." She flashed him a grin that held more than a little satisfaction, then headed for the door. "Just let me get a few things from the car, then we can get to work."

David watched her leave and heard her footsteps on the plank, then on the dock. As the sound died out, he turned and glanced around the room, Daniel's room. Yet as he ran his hand over his face, welcoming the roughness of a coming beard to the silk he'd felt moments earlier, he knew the room felt as if Carin had taken it over.

All he had to do was inhale to catch a trace of the gentle sweetness that seemed to cling to her. He glanced at the bed. Why did it seem like a lifetime since he'd had the nightmare? The nightmare. For the past few minutes, he'd forgotten about it completely, but now, it was there again.

With the book clutched in his hand, he went into the tiny kitchen and got a small bottle of water out of the refrigerator. He laid the notebook on the counter, twisted the top off the bottle, then drank the entire contents.

As he dropped the bottle in the wastebasket near the cupboard, he looked down at the book. He hadn't told Carin everything, that Daniel's notes weren't just important, they were priceless to him.

David felt his stomach tighten. He picked up the notebook and knew that Daniel wouldn't have dropped them or forgotten them, unless something had happened to make him.

He heard the door close and he knew that Carin was at the doorway to the kitchen. "Let's get started," she said.

He looked away from the book to the doorway. She was clutching a slender briefcase. She looked excited, as if she was about to embark on some remarkable adventure. He wished he felt like that. "Yes, let's get started," he said and headed toward her.

But she didn't move to let him pass. She held out her free hand to him. "The book?"

He handed it to her without a word, and when she walked away to go to the bed, he headed for the desk. Sorting through the clutter, he found a yellow highlighter. "Use this to mark anything you find that can help," he said as he turned to find Carin sitting on the edge of the bed, her briefcase open. He watched her take out a pair of red-framed glasses, then scoot back on the bed until she was sitting against the headboard. When she tucked her feet under her, she looked up at him. "Excuse me?"

"This highlighter," he said, crossing to hold it out to her, hoping the glasses would diminish whatever it was that made his breath catch when he looked at her.

She put on her glasses, then looked up at him. "Thanks," she said and took the highlighter from him. One glance from her blue eyes through the lenses chased all his hopes. They only made her eyes seem bigger and emphasized the delicate definition of her facial structure. *So much for that hope,* he thought as he turned from the sight of her getting comfortable on the bed he'd just left.

He crossed to lift a clutter of magazines off one of the chairs that faced the draped windows. Then he sank down on the cushions and pushed his feet out in front of him. While he stared at the closed drapes, every part of him seemed centered on any movement or sound from Carin. When the bed shifted and Carin finally spoke up, it was a relief. "David?"

He glanced over at her, the bright overhead light reflecting off her glasses. "Did you find something?"

"I don't know. It's all confusing. Your brother's mind runs in circles. There are bits and pieces, phrases and ideas. It would take a detective to make sense out of all of this." She hesitated and took off her glasses. "Hey, maybe that's the answer."

"The answer?"

"Hank. He's a private detective." She was sitting up straight now. "He'd be perfect."

How could this women generate so much energy when it was...? He looked at the clock. It was almost one a.m. And the idea of an ex-fiancé being brought in on this was very distasteful to David—far from perfect. "What could I tell this *Hank* to help him find Daniel? If I knew what to tell him, I could find him myself."

Carin frowned, nibbling on the earpiece of her glasses, then her eyes widened. "He could trace his credit cards?"

That almost made David laugh. "Daniel hated getting a driver's license, much less getting tied to credit. He pays cash for everything."

She sank back against the headboard, slipped on her glasses again and read. "What do you make of this— Hell's Way, Trig, Manta, Tar, Scat?"

"Doesn't ring a bell."

"Or, listen to this. 'The shadow was as mysterious as the Arizona hills that hide the source of life-giving water.' It sounds like he had a wonderfully vivid imagination and poetic mind."

"Or maybe he was just rambling. Too bad he didn't write down something like, 'On day one I drove west until I hit Tucson,' or something else we could make sense of."

"What do you think Hell's Way is, a town?"

David glanced over at the desk and spotted a thick atlas. He grabbed the heavy book, then went to the bed and sank down on the side by Carin. He flipped to the index of Arizona, then ran his finger down the names of towns. "No Hell's Way."

Carin scooted nearer to David to hold out the notebook. In bright yellow she'd marked, "Hell's Way. Use it or not? Could be great atmosphere and character."

He could feel her body heat. He determinedly stared at the highlighted text. "Anything else about it?"

"I haven't found anything else."

David went back to the desk to drop the atlas on the other books. Then he turned to find Carin bent over the notebook, her hair falling like a silvery veil to partially hide her face. "There has to be something in that book," he murmured. "Something we can use."

Carin looked up, and her blue eyes behind the lenses were even more unsettling. "Do you have any idea at all what Daniel could be doing?" she asked.

"He's on the Harley, probably pretending he's T. J. Pierce. He does that. He lives what the character is going to live in the book so it's valid on the written page. He and his bike. Off into the wild blue yonder."

"You can't think of anyone he'd stop to see, any place he'd visit when he was done with the research?"

"Daniel did his research and..." His words trailed off as he remembered that Daniel did indeed have one pattern that he knew about, and it didn't do anything to alleviate his concern.

"And?" she prodded.

"And he comes right back here, before he forgets anything." His voice was flat as he furrowed his brow.

"Another broken pattern," she said softly.

"Yes, a broken pattern," he admitted. He'd never felt so frustrated and tense in his life. "How about a drink?"

"Tequila?" she asked, and he could have sworn there was a shadow of a smile playing around her lips.

"That was a bad judgment call at a party the last night of the dig. What I need right now is coffee."

"Coffee sounds good." She scooted back on the bed, the briefcase by her side, and started reading the notebook again.

David turned from her, from that look of concentration on her face and the way her hair tumbled forward. It took five minutes to heat up the water, make instant coffee and find some sugar and powdered creamer.

When he walked back into the room with a steaming mug of coffee in each hand, he stopped just inside the doorway. Carin was still on the bed, but she'd shifted lower, her head to one side, her blond hair pale against the dark blue of the sheets. She was asleep, her lashes dark arcs against her cheeks, and the notebook was laid by her briefcase.

David crossed to put the coffee on the bedside table, then looked down at her. "Dr. Walker?" She didn't move. "Carin?"

She stirred slightly, then settled back into the pillows. As David watched her, her lashes fluttered, then she sighed. So beautiful in sleep, and so full of ideas and opinions when she was awake. David almost smiled at the idea of a sleeping beauty, then glanced at the clock.

Almost two o'clock. The idea of her being in the bed he'd left earlier was unsettling, but he wouldn't awaken her. He'd learned earlier when he'd cupped her chin what it felt like to touch her. No contact. No matter how appealing it was when he watched her sigh again, and the way her breasts stirred the silk of her blouse.

He turned from the sight of her. Just too damned appealing. He snapped off the sidelight, then took his mug of coffee and crossed to turn off the overhead lights. In the soft semidarkness, he went silently to the curtained doors that opened onto the observation deck. He tugged back the heavy white material to expose the view of the marina with its night-lights and the lights from the docked boats, glowing orbs in the darkness and on the water.

In the distance, he saw where the marina opened into the bay, where dark, silent waters reflected lights and the glow of a high moon and a scattering of stars. It was the same sky that had been over Mexico last night when he'd laughed and joked with the students and shared their tequila. But life had changed dramatically in twenty-four hours.

He glanced back at Carin in the shadows of the bed, and conceded it had changed very dramatically. He moved abruptly to the chair facing the doors, and sank down low enough on the cushions to rest his head against the back. He took a sip of the now tepid coffee, then put the mug on the floor by the chair and stared out at the night.

When Carin sighed, he closed his eyes and tried to relax. Weariness flowed over him, and he knew he needed sleep to be able to think clearly in the morning. He pushed his feet out in front of him and rested his hands on the chair arms.

In the morning he'd figure out what to do, how to go about finding Daniel. He felt sleep flutter around him. In the morning everything would make sense, even Carin being here.

THE DREAM CAME from nowhere, accompanied by a bone-deep chill and a soft whooshing sound from a great distance off. Everything was dark and still, yet he knew there were people around, moving cautiously, almost in a sad manner. "Too bad," he thought he heard someone say, yet the voice was nebulous, more a suggestion in his mind than actual words. "So sad," the voice whispered, and he felt a skimming touch on his forehead.

There was absolute darkness, even though his eyes were open. And the cold increased as the touch withdrew. "It looks bad. Do you think he'll make it?" another voice asked. A man this time. It had to be a man, yet it came from the same source as the first voice.

David struggled to move, but he couldn't. There was a weight on his chest that stopped him from breathing. He tried to take in air, then suddenly the weight lifted and air rushed into his lungs. The next second, the weight was back, heavy and oppressive, then gone, giving him air again.

"Who is he?" the first voice asked, soft and so close that David knew if he could see, he'd be looking into the speaker's face.

"No idea. It's awful to die alone," the man said.

"I'm not dying," David wanted to yell.

"He's got a chance to make it," the female voice said.

"Yes, yes," David screamed in his mind. "Listen to her. I'll make it."

The touch was on his forehead again, as wispy as an errant breeze. "You won't die alone," the woman whispered, echoing in his mind. "I won't let you."

"I'm not dying!" he screamed. "I'm not. I'm not!"

In a violent rush he was awake, sitting bolt upright in the chair, with his own internal screams still echoing in his mind. Someone was touching him, hands were on his arm, warm against the cold, as if the dream had invaded reality.

"Are you all right?" Softly whispered words. "David?"

He turned and saw that Carin was crouched by the chair, inches from him, her hair in wild disarray, her eyes still heavy from sleep, but touched with concern. The sensation of her hand on his bare arm helped him focus past his own rapid breathing and the shock of waking so abruptly.

The touch seemed to anchor him in this world of reality, refusing to let him slip back into the world of nightmares. But as Carin moved even closer, so close he could feel her breath brush his face, he knew she couldn't be his anchor.

He moved back, pulling his arm free of her hold as he sat forward. With his elbows on his knees, he rested his head in his hands. "Sorry about that," he muttered.

"What happened?" Carin was close to him, and for a minute he wanted her to touch him again, to ground him and keep him in the reality of this moment. If he held her and buried his face in her silky warmth, maybe all the nightmares would flee. Or maybe it would open a whole new Pandora's box.

"What happened?" he echoed without chancing a look at her.

"I heard you call out, as if you were talking to someone, yelling at them. I couldn't make it out, but it woke me."

He dropped his hands and sat back in the chair, finally looking at Carin who was still crouched by the chair, her hands holding onto the wicker arm. "A dream. That's all. Just a dream."

"Do you have dreams like this a lot?"

He exhaled and rested his head against the back of the chair. "Never. Not until . . ." He saw the way she was studying him, the same way she had earlier, the way a doctor would look at a patient she was paid to help.

"Until when?" she prodded softly.

"Until I overdid it with tequila. I'm not a great drinker." He finally noticed that dawn was here, streaking pinks and purples over the water of the marina. He glanced at the clock—6:15. He'd slept most of the night—until the dream. He glanced back at Carin, her deep blue eyes narrowed, studying him. "I actually never dream," he heard himself say.

"Of course you do," she said as she stood slowly and smoothed her blouse that had come free of the waistband of her slacks. "Everyone dreams. It's humanly impossible to sleep without dreaming at least five times a night. You aren't any different. You just choose not to remember what dreams you have."

"It's not a choice," he muttered as he stood. If he had that choice he wouldn't be remembering the dream he'd just endured, or think he could hear that soft voice that had come to him in the dream if he only stood absolutely still and listened.

Before she could say anything else, he picked up his mug by the chair, then turned back to Carin. Dawn was at her back, its pastel colors haloing her as she combed her hair back from her face with her fingers. For that instant the sweep of her neck was exposed, the delicate line of her jaw, then her hair fell in a pale cloud around her face.

"Is that from last night?" she asked as she glanced at the mug.

"Yeah. You were asleep." He didn't want to think of watching her in the bed. "I'll make some fresh for both of us." he said as he headed into the kitchen.

"I could use some. I'm not really a morning person," she called after him.

As he heated the water and mixed up the coffee, he tried to shake off the lingering wisps of the dream. Death. Why would he be suddenly contemplating his mortality? Why would he be having dreams that held a life of their own, refusing to drift off when daylight came?

He stirred the coffee into the hot water, then headed back into the cabin. "I never found out last night if you use sugar or cream. There's some in—"

He stopped just inside the doorway when he saw the room was empty and the door to the dock steps was ajar. Fresh air invaded the room, touched with the cool crispness of the morning. Carin was gone.

He stood in the empty room, unsettled by feeling as if he'd been deserted when he should have felt relieved that he could figure out what to do without Carin's interference or her constant ideas. But before he could assimilate how he felt, she came rushing back in, a tote bag in her hand.

"If you don't mind, I'll freshen up." She swung the door shut, then turned to look at David. "Is that all right with you?"

"Sure," he said, feeling as if he was on a roller coaster. Relief that she hadn't left abruptly shouldn't be leaving him vaguely dizzy. And when she crossed to him, took one of the mugs, flashed him a bright smile and said, "Thanks," he shouldn't have been so aware of the slight contact of her cold fingers on his hand.

She turned and walked to the bathroom door, but stopped to glance back at David. "I'll only be a few minutes, then you can tell me where you're going to start looking for your brother."

The relief was evaporating very quickly. "I'm not going anywhere. I'm staying here to wait for Daniel to call or to come back."

The smile was replaced by a look of surprise, then she came back to where David stood. She looked up at him and demanded, "Stay here? Just do nothing? I thought—"

"You thought what? That I'd have some sort of psychic experience and it would tell me where to find him?"

She just stared at him.

"Oh, no you don't." He shook his head. "Don't you dare suggest hypnosis or some sort of drug therapy to unlock my psychic potential."

"I don't use drug therapy, but you know all the terms, don't you?"

"I know all the gibberish. And believe me, it won't happen. If I find my brother, it's going to be the product of logic and work."

"I agree."

He stared at her. "What?"

"I agree. If you find Daniel you'll do it your way."

"Absolutely," he said, but his conviction was wavering.

"All right. Tell me how you're going to do it?"

As she asked the question, he knew the answer. He'd probably known it since finding the notebook. "Did you get to the back of his notes?"

She nodded.

"And?"

"He wrote something about T. J. finally getting a life, and he knew just how he was going to give it to him."

"Do you think his research was finished?"

She shrugged. "It seemed as if it was."

"If that's the case, then he must have been heading back when he lost the notebook. He's got that map, references to places and things. I think I'll try to recreate his route and see what I can find."

"Recreate it, or follow it?"

"Both," he said.

"Great! Good going. You'd make Sam Spade proud. Now, how are you going to get there?"

"I'll rent a car and start driving, following any pattern I can pick up, and see if anything develops."

She dropped the tote bag on the floor to cradle the cup of coffee in both hands. As she took a sip, she eyed him over the rim of the steaming mug. "Are you open to a suggestion?"

He didn't know just what he was open to anymore. "It depends. What is it?"

"I'm going to Albuquerque by the lowest southern route, the one Daniel started out on, and you're welcome to come along with me."

Now that she was back and this close, he didn't think being in a car with her would be a smart thing. "Thanks, but I—"

"Listen to me. I know the southwestern states. I was brought up in New Mexico, and I've spent a lot of time in Arizona."

"I'm not sure—"

She cut right in. "And Daniel's talked to me about this new book. Maybe something will jog my memory and help in the search."

Carin watched David, knowing how reluctant he was to let her in. But she wanted to see this through to the end. "Why are you doing this?" he asked, the clear light of morning cutting deep shadows under his cheekbones and throat.

She shrugged. "I'm worried. I'm going that way. I've got a car." She looked away to sip more coffee, avoiding direct eye contact for a moment. Everything she'd said was the truth, but it was also true that if she was around David longer, she might be able to find out if he had some tie with his brother, something that even he didn't know about. Or a tie that he wouldn't admit to.

She knew from the short time she'd been around him that David had a strong persona. He seemed to dominate any place he occupied. She held more tightly onto the cup before touching her chin where he'd held her last night. "Believe me, I know that route," she said quickly. "I've traveled it a lot."

"But you've got a schedule, and I don't have a clue how long this is going to take."

She shrugged. "I've got a week before I have to make my appointment. I was going to visit with my family before that, and I'm sure they wouldn't mind if I'm a few days late. And I'm driving."

"All the way to Albuquerque?"

"Yes."

"Why aren't you flying?"

"I don't fly. I don't like it."

He actually smiled at that, an expression that eased the lines in his face and made her almost feel as if the sun had flooded the room. "A shrink who's afraid to fly?" he murmured.

"I'm not a shrink, I'm a research psychologist, and—"

"And you're not afraid to fly?"

"No, I'm not. I just don't like it. That's all."

She could feel her face heating up, not helped at all by the disbelieving look he was giving her. "Sure, and Mount Vesuvius was a little firecracker."

She lifted her chin, meeting his gaze. "I'm not perfect, Mr. Hart. Believe me. I've got phobias, like I hate flying, I'm mildly claustrophobic, and I hate snakes. I'm a compulsive talker. I can't look at anything with sour cream on it without getting sick, and I've been told, I'm a bit obsessive about my work."

"What's that all supposed to mean?"

"It means, I might be a psychologist, but I'm still a human being with flaws and phobias. But, *this* human being has a perfectly good car sitting at the end of the dock which she's glad to share with you, if you want to take her up on the offer."

She had never in her life reeled off all her shortcomings to anyone, let alone a man who already thought she was off center. And from the way he was looking at her, she couldn't tell if he was ready to throw her out or take her up on the offer of a ride.

He pushed his hands in the pockets of his slacks, then rocked forward on the balls of his feet. "You've made your case. How soon can you be ready to leave?"

"Give me ten minutes," she said, reaching for her tote and hurrying into the bathroom.

"DID YOU FIGURE OUT anything from his notes?" Carin asked David as they left San Diego behind an hour later.

David shifted in the leather bucket seat of the brand-new red BMW convertible and closed Daniel's notebook before he looked at her. He wasn't about to tell her he was trying to figure out why he was doing this and why he'd agreed to her offer. It might have been the rational thing to do at the time, but it certainly wasn't the smart thing.

Just looking at Carin in the clear August sun underscored the fact he should have found a rental car and come alone. She'd changed into white shorts, white sandals and a hot-pink tank top, then twisted her hair on top of her head and tugged a white cotton baseball cap over it. The brim shaded part of her face, and oversize sunglasses hid her eyes. Wispy curls escaped the confines of the cap, and she swiped at tendrils that tickled her cheek.

Her skin was smooth and faintly tanned, her legs seemed to go on forever, and all in all, as David looked at her, he thought that Carin Walker looked very Californian, very yuppie and very sexy.

She slanted him a look from behind the glasses. "Well, did you figure out anything?"

He looked down at the small notebook in his hand and paraphrased his original conclusion. "I just figured out that this is a stupid thing to do."

"Why's it stupid?"

"It's like looking for a needle in a haystack. I would have had a better chance of finding Daniel by going with my original plan of staying at his place and waiting for a phone call."

"From whom?"

"From Daniel or anyone." He looked away from her to the lightly traveled freeway, then to groups of tract homes to the south, backed by low hills covered with drought-resistant chaparral and a scattering of spreading oaks. "Tell me, how in the hell am I ever going to find him doing this?"

"I told you, he mentioned this route to me. He asked me all sorts of questions about it and told me he was going on the low route all the way to New Mexico. And we have his notes. Surely we can figure out something from them."

"And what if he passes us heading home?"

"Do you think he will?"

The answer came without rhyme or reason, and it shook him that it came so clearly. Daniel wouldn't be passing them going home. David tried to deny the certainty of his statement, but he couldn't. "I don't know," he hedged, rubbing the bridge of his nose with his forefinger.

"We can call his place whenever we stop," she offered.

"I planned on it."

"That's settled. Now why don't you look through the notebook some more and see what we can put together?"

Chapter Four

David flipped the notebook open and skimmed over the first two or three pages. "Okay, figure out Hell's Way, Trig, Manta, Tar, Scat. Could it be a new version of the seven dwarfs?"

"No, but the words mean *some*thing," Carin said, missing the joke.

He skipped to a portion she'd highlighted. "Shadows ... still there, Coyote Creek, Lizard Sands."

"Places?"

"I checked the map of Arizona and New Mexico while you were taking your shower, and none of them is there."

"Maybe they're nicknames, sort of like a town that's had a lot of earthquakes being called Tremor Flats."

"So we're looking for some town that's got a reason to be called Lizard Sands?"

She cast him a fleeting glance accompanied by a suggestion of a smile. "Sort of conjures up horrible images, doesn't it?"

"It does."

"Too bad Daniel didn't do his notes chronologically, rather than in waves of impressions."

"Yeah, too bad," he murmured, closing the notebook.

"Even so, we can conclude that Daniel wrote about where he'd been, places he went through. So, if we find those places, and if we can prove he's been there, we can keep going."

"Perfect logic," he murmured.

She shrugged, her slender shoulders moving in a sharp movement that looked a bit like an angry gesture. "Even *I'm* capable of logic from time to time."

"I actually thought doctors of any sort were chained to logic."

"Chained is a bad choice of words, but logic is the basis for everything."

He shifted to look at her more clearly and asked something that had been eating at him since he'd found out why she knew Daniel. "I assume you got your M.D. and that you interned, since you're a psychologist. That's a lot of years, and a lot of expense."

"It was."

"So why are you wasting all of that training and your time checking into this psychic link theory?"

"Why did you spend, I think Daniel said it was a month, of your time digging in one spot just to find a piece of broken pottery that might prove that some second-level civilization probably existed aeons ago?" She kept looking straight ahead. "You obviously spent plenty of time getting your education and working on your postgraduate studies."

"Because I had a piece of pottery that I could touch to validate my theory."

He didn't miss the color creeping into her cheeks, or the way her hands tightened on the wheel. "You don't accept anything that you can't see, touch, taste, hear or smell, do you?"

"I didn't say that."

"That's exactly what you're saying. You dig up a bone or a pot or a disintegrating heap of stones that could have been a wall, and you find actual, physical proof that what you've only theorized up until then, is fact."

"That's the idea."

"Well, I theorize that when two people come from the same egg, from the identical origin, there is a distinct possibility that there can be some connection that goes beyond what you can see or feel or taste or hear or smell. That's not crazy. It's not farfetched."

"It's not?"

She sat back, flexing her hand on the steering wheel, and exhaled in a rush. "No, it's not. I've worked with twins separated by a whole continent, yet when one broke his leg, the other twin experienced pain and weakness in the same leg almost at the same moment of the other's accident. What would you call that?"

"A coincidence?"

"Well, I think it's more than that. I've dealt with case after case of similar circumstances."

"I told you Daniel used to lie about his experiences."

"He was a child playing games."

"And adults don't play games?"

"Of course they do. Adults also close themselves off to experiences that they can't explain. They hide from them, just the way anyone in eighteenth-century Salem would have hid any unusual, inexplicable experience they had. No one wanted to be burned at the stake.''

"They outlawed burning at the stake years ago,'' he murmured.

She looked right at him, the expression in her eyes hidden by the dark lenses. But judging from the set of her mouth and the angle of her chin, David knew he should probably be thankful he wasn't taking the full impact of those eyes. "They obviously didn't outlaw closed-mindedness or prejudice or stupidity.''

David felt the impact of her words, as clearly as if she had slapped him across the face. And he knew that she would have loved to do that very thing, but being civilized, she'd chosen words instead. "You see me as closed-minded, prejudiced and stupid?''

The car sped up. "No, of course you're not stupid.''

David shook his head, swallowing the laughter that suddenly rose in his throat. She was sharp. Grudgingly he admitted to himself that Carin Walker wasn't just another crazy who believed in voodoo. She was an intelligent woman who believed in it. But the question of why was eating at him.

He ran a hand roughly over his face, then glanced at the desert they were heading into. Barren, dry land stretched out on either side. Off in the distance, low hills were blurred by a morning haze. "All right. You've made your point.''

"I hope so,'' she said, and the car gained more speed as traffic became nonexistent on the four-lane road.

"Without danger of getting into any more trouble with you, can I ask you something that I'm just curious about?"

"What?"

"Why are you trying to prove the unprovable?"

"I've always been fascinated by it."

"And someone gave you money to do that?"

"I've got funds."

"Who funds you?"

"An interested party."

"Such as?"

She sped up even more. "Someone interested in proving the unprovable."

"Wouldn't it be easier to say you don't want to tell me whose money you're using?"

She tugged on the bill of her cap with one hand, then placed her left elbow on the door, letting her fingers rest lightly on the steering wheel. "Okay. I don't want to tell you."

"Why?"

"Now, that's why I didn't just say it like that the first time."

"Why?"

"You don't accept any answer I give you about anything."

"I do too."

"No, you don't. You could have said, 'All right, you don't want to tell me,' but you didn't. Not any more than you accepted anything I said back at the houseboat without questioning it."

"Then just let's stick to facts."

"Boy, am I for that," she breathed.

"We finally agree on something." He shifted in his seat. "So, where are we going exactly?"

"We'll follow this freeway to the border, through Yuma and keep going from there. I usually drive straight through to Tucson before I stop for the night, but we can stop anytime you say. We also need to start looking for restaurants."

"I'm not hungry," he said, with food the farthest thing from his mind at the moment.

"Neither am I . . . yet. But I told Daniel about some places along the way that I stopped to eat, and he said he'd try one of them. I thought it would be logical to check them as we go."

"Eminently logical," David murmured.

"To show you how logical I am, look in my briefcase."

He turned and picked up the thin briefcase off the backseat, laid it on his legs and unzipped the closure. Right on top of a loose-leaf binder were two pictures of Daniel. One was a small publicity shot from the back cover of his books, and the other one was a two-by-three snapshot that David had seen on his brother's desk before. It was of Daniel on his bike, his hair long, his eyes squinting into the sun.

"Well?" she asked.

"I didn't even think about photos," he admitted.

"I got them while you were getting dressed. Do I get points for logic?"

He put them in Daniel's notebook, then closed her briefcase and put it back on the rear seat. As he settled, he looked at Carin. "Give yourself a point."

"Thanks." She motioned to the glove compartment. "There's lotion and sunglasses in there if you need them."

He liked the sun, and after a month in Mexico, he was past burning. "I'm fine." He glanced at her fair skin. "But don't you burn?"

She ran one slender hand over her bare shoulder and down her arm. "Sometimes. I started wearing hats and sunscreen when I got the convertible." She glanced at David. "If you'd like I can put up the top. I meant to ask you at the houseboat, but forgot about it."

"No, it's fine." Having the top down and the air rushing past was one way of dealing with this woman's presence. For now, David had no wish to be in a closed car with her. "Is this convertible a product of your claustrophobia?"

"Probably. I never analyzed it that far." Carin pressed the accelerator. "More likely it's because there is nothing like the freedom of driving through the desert with the top down when there aren't any other cars on the road."

David glanced at the speedometer. "You won't stay free long if a cop clocks you at ninety miles an hour."

She immediately eased off the gas. "I'm so used to this route that I forget about the speed." She motioned to the notebook on David's lap. "Why don't you read aloud from the notebook? Sometimes when you hear yourself speak words, your mind perceives them differently. You read, and I'll watch for the restaurants."

David flipped open the notebook and as the car sped along the freeway toward the California-Arizona border, he read Daniel's notes out loud.

"T.J. Pierce, what motivation? What thoughts when facing the curse? A quest? A crisis? The long road of discovery. Southwest, Arizona, New Mexico. Character. Infusion of character. Why would Pierce leave security for the unknown? Thoughts on this subject or risk taking and..."

Carin listened to David read his brother's notes, his deep rough-edged voice like a chant in her ears as she kept her eyes open for the restaurants. The knots that had invaded her stomach during their argument were easing and she didn't want them to come back. Just because David didn't agree with her, didn't make him an enemy. Truth was truth. She knew the truth of what she spoke about, whether he accepted it or not.

She regripped the steering wheel and inhaled, filling her lungs with the hot desert air. She'd put down some quick notes this morning while David had been showering and dressing. Notes about two brothers, two human beings, part of each other, yet separate and different. And David really was very different from Daniel. Their looks were echoes of each other in a basic way, but deep down, the fantasy and joy in Daniel had been redefined as reality and maddening self-assurance in David.

She watched the road ahead, trying to focus on David's voice, and unconsciously rubbing her fingers over her chin. She didn't usually argue with anyone. Hadn't her mother told her often enough that she was the peacemaker, the one who didn't need to prove a point to someone who didn't understand? David certainly burst that myth.

She squinted as she tried to make out the signs that shimmered in the heat by the side of the freeway, but her mind was elsewhere. So, David was a realist. He believed what he could prove with his senses. And what if David really didn't have a link with Daniel? What if he was absolutely right about that?

Or what if he wasn't? She knew that was the main reason she was in this car now. She could have walked away, she could have insisted on calling the police or leaving David at Daniel's to wait for his brother. But as David's voice seemed to fill all the spaces around her, she knew she wanted to be here. She wanted to watch David, to study him and see what happened.

"A true scientist," her sister had said. "You never leave a what-if alone."

She glanced at David as the wind tousled his hair. He looked tanned against the whiteness of his shirt. His jeans were clean and pressed, but he still looked comfortable and casual. The man disturbed her in more ways than the fact that their ideas were at opposite poles. He disturbed her in a basic way that she could only call awareness. If he moved, she was aware of it. If he took a deep breath, she heard it even over the rushing wind in the convertible.

She realized that her penchant for what-ifs could extend far beyond this study with David . . . if she let them. Thankfully she was saved from delving into those what-ifs when she spotted a billboard for the first restaurant she'd told Daniel about.

THREE HOURS LATER they were within fifty miles of the Arizona-California border and had stopped at two restaurants where no one remembered seeing Daniel. David had tucked the pictures back in the notebook, and for the past ten miles, the silence in the car had been almost tangible. He sat with the notebook in his hand, his eyes on the landscape they were passing. Carin could feel tension building in her neck and shoulders.

"Can I ask you something?" she said, welcoming the sound of her own voice.

David shifted in the seat. "What is it?"

"This character that your brother writes about . . ."

"T. J. Pierce."

"I thought T. J. Pierce was supposed to be a private investigator?"

"He is."

"From what's in the notebook, I don't see any planning of a mystery in this book. It's all random impressions and images of discovery and self-realization."

"Daniel always said the mystery was the easy part to write, but the growth in Pierce was what stopped him over and over again. He didn't see the man as a vacuum, or just a killing machine. He thought that life was growth and he wanted to show that in his writing."

"Has he?"

"You haven't read any of the books?"

"I've heard about them from a lot of people, and I bought one, but I've been so busy, I didn't get to it yet," she said.

"T. J. Pierce rides a Harley, just like Daniel's. He lives in a trailer at the beach, sort of like Daniel. He's a detective who does things his own way—he kills the bad guys one minute and searches for the meaning of life the next."

"He sounds like a complicated man," she murmured, then spotted the sign for Blakeney, a small town just ahead. "But I guess life's like that, one complication after another."

As she slowed and pulled onto the ramp to head for the frontage road, she felt David watching her. "It sure is," he said.

Carin pulled onto the side road, turned west and drove parallel to the freeway where dusty fields of scrub and weeds were on the right and a six-foot chain-link fence to the left.

"Where are we going now?" David asked.

"Another restaurant." She glanced at him, the bright, hot sun clearly etching his features in its glow, but shadowing his eyes. "Are you hungry yet?"

He checked the digital clock on the dash. "It's almost noon. I guess I could use something to eat."

She motioned ahead of them about half a mile down the road on the right side to a twenty-foot wooden sign in the shape of a cactus with Willy's Mirage splashed in red across deep green. A folding sign under it on the shoulder of the road advertised Gas, Diesel, Good Food and Cold Beer.

"It doesn't look like much, but the food really is good," she said.

"It's not a mirage?"

She flashed him a smile. "No. I always thought a real mirage would look beautiful and inviting. That's not Willy's."

Willy's Mirage was a dreary-looking place, consisting of a squat building fronting barren, heat-burned fields, with gas pumps off to one side and two huge oaks that partially shaded the restaurant's flat roof and oxidized-red siding. Most of the shade that touched the packed-earth parking lot was taken by about a half-dozen big rigs. Two more diesel trucks were at the pumps to the left.

"How did you ever find this place?" David asked.

"I got off the freeway by mistake one time. I didn't know that Blakeney is farther down, two exits more. But I needed gas and saw the sign, so I got the gas and stayed to eat. I wasn't disappointed."

"And you told Daniel about it?"

"I mentioned it. I said if he wanted something that had plenty of substance but little style, Willy's might be as good a place for him to stop as any."

As she slowed to turn into the parking lot, she spotted a space big enough for the BMW on the far side of a chicken transporter in the shade of one of the oaks. She headed for it. "Isn't there an old saying about truckers knowing the best places to eat?"

"Or they've been on the road too long."

"Trust me, the food's really good," she said as she parked in the relative coolness of the shade.

"Look at those," David said, motioning to two motorcycles by the trunk of the ancient oak. "Is there an old saying for motorcycles, too?"

"Not that I know of," she said as she grabbed her purse and got out. She looked at the motorcycles, bright red, brand-new and shiny with chrome. "I never saw Daniel's bike. What's it like?"

David moved closer to the bikes. "Not like these. They look like some kid's toys." He looked at Carin, his eyes narrowed by the glare of the sun. "Daniel's is a '55 Harley, modified by its original owner into what's called a chopper."

"It sounds as if Daniel's motorcycle's a collector's item."

"For some it would be, but for Daniel it's a passion."

"A passion. That sounds..."

"Dramatic?"

"I guess so."

"It's not. To feel passion, you have to hate with as much feeling as you love."

"I never got the idea that Daniel hated anything," she said.

He ran a hand around the back of his neck. "Daniel hates any form of confinement. And he gets real freedom riding the bike. That's why he does his research that way. It isn't because he has to, but he needs to. He needs spells where he can ride down the road and feel the wind rushing past. It sort of balances out the time he needs to spend inside writing, so he can..."

"Ride down the road and be free," she finished.

He nodded. "Exactly. And that bike is his getaway machine. His passion."

She felt the dampness of her clothes against her hot skin. "Do you have the pictures?"

He held up the notebook. "Right in here." He turned toward the restaurant. "Let's get inside where it's cool and see what we can find out."

She hurried after him, falling in step as he approached the entrance. They walked under the deep overhang that shaded the series of windows along the front of the restaurant. David reached for the door and tugged it open to let Carin go inside ahead of him.

As she started past him, she hesitated and looked up at David. The heat was filming his skin with moisture and his hair was clinging damply to his temples and neck. "Did you ever ride his motorcycle?"

"A few times."

"Did you like it?"

"It didn't become a passion with me." He met her gaze without blinking. "A machine just doesn't engender that sort of response in me." Carin looked away from him, knowing there was no reason to wonder just what would evoke passion in David.

She stepped into the chill of the air-conditioned restaurant, into a large low-ceilinged room filled with the clatter of glass on glass, piped-in country music and the mingled odor of coffee, frying foods and age. Booths lined the walls on both sides, small tables were scattered in the middle of a brown linoleum floor and a counter ran the length of the back with the kitchen visible through a cutout in the wall.

She sensed David behind her, then he was so close that she felt his breath tickle the sensitive spot by her ear. "There're pay phones over there. I'll be right back."

Then he was gone. She turned and saw him striding across the room to the far side near a group of cigarette machines and a bank of phones. He stopped by the first phone, put change in it, then dialed a number. She knew he was calling Daniel, since he'd called at every stop they'd made.

And when he turned back to her, she knew he'd reached the machine again. His face was tight and as he came close to her, he shook his head. "Nothing."

"We've only been gone a few hours," she said. "We'll keep trying."

"Sure," he murmured.

She looked away from him and crossed to the cash register to her left. A young girl sat on a stool behind a small counter cluttered with displays for gum and candy. The dark-haired girl couldn't have been more than sixteen and wore a tight dress in red-checkered cotton. She motioned to the room at large with a sweep of her hand. "Welcome to Willy's. Sit where ever you'd like."

Carin felt David touch her on her shoulder, his touch cool on her hot skin, and he spoke close to her ear again. "How about a booth?"

"Sure," she said, quickly moving away from the contact and toward the nearest empty booth on the left side of the room. She slid onto the hard vinyl seat, putting her purse on the table, then rubbed at goose bumps on her arms. Surely they came from the chill in the room, and not from that moment of heat when David had leaned so close to her.

She looked at David as he settled opposite her, and she was thankful he wasn't looking at her. His hazel eyes scanned the noisy room that was almost half full of customers and a faint frown tugged at his eyebrows. He said something, but it was too low for Carin to make out the words.

"Excuse me?"

"This place," David said more loudly as he glanced at her. "It's the sort of place Daniel would get a kick out of coming to."

A waitress came over to the table, a tall and heavy-set woman in the same style dress as the girl at the counter wore. But on this woman it looked restrictive, and the buttons down the front seemed to strain to keep together. Bright red lipstick looked stark against pale freckled skin, and bleached blond hair had been teased into an improbable bouffant.

She flashed a toothy smile at the two of them, plopped menus down on the table and said, "I'm Stella. Can I get you a cold drink while you're looking at the menu?"

"Iced tea with lemon," Carin said.

She scribbled on her pad, then turned to David. "And you?"

"The same. One more thing." David took out the pictures of Daniel and laid them on top of his closed menu. "I was wondering if you've seen this man?"

She leaned closer and squinted at the pictures, then drew back. "What's this, some joke or something?"

"No, it's not, I just—"

She frowned at David. "That's you, big as life and twice as natural. What's the joke?"

Carin broke in. "It's not a joke. The man in the picture is this man's identical twin. They've lost touch and the last he heard he was heading this way. He might have stopped here for a bite to eat."

The woman looked from David to the pictures, then back to David. "He's your brother?"

"Yes, he is."

"When was he supposed to be around here?"

"He might have come sometime in the last half of June."

"I wouldn't be knowing anything about then. I've only been working here for a week."

"Is there anyone here who would have been here then?" David asked.

She shrugged. "Lou the cook and maybe Willy the owner. They've both been here forever."

"Can we talk to Lou or Willy?"

"Lou's gone for a few days, but Willy's around, just not working today."

"Is there any way we could talk to Willy?"

"Boy, I don't know. We're not supposed to bother Willy at home."

"Let me put that another way," Carin said as she reached in her purse and took out her wallet. She slipped a five-dollar bill out and laid it on the table in front of her. Then she looked up at the waitress. "How about just giving up a phone number or an address and we'll take it from there?"

Stella eyed the money. "I don't know...."

Carin took out another five, put it on top of the first one, and pushed both bills toward the waitress. "Trust me. We'll take all the flack. We won't say where we got the information. But we need to talk to Willy."

The woman said, "What the hell," as she reached for the money. "Give me a couple of minutes." She folded the bills and tucked them into her cleavage. "I'll find out what I can do for you, but I can't promise anything."

"That's fine. We'd appreciate anything you can do."

As the waitress hurried away to the back of the restaurant, David touched the back of Carin's hand. The contact was light and cool against her skin, and as she turned, she glanced at his hand. His fingers were strong and tanned, with square, short nails. Not the hand of a professor, she thought as she looked at David.

"Ten dollars?" he asked.

She tried to ignore the way his hand felt over hers, and made light of what was going on. "I don't have any idea what the going rate is for buying information," she said, her hand very still under his. "Hank never did tell me that."

"He didn't give you a crash course in bribery?"

She shrugged. "He gave me a crash course in many things, but not that. What do *you* know about bribery?"

He smiled, and she thought that he looked so much better without that perpetual frown tugging at his features. "Not much, but if you have to do that very often, we'll be broke."

"Isn't it worth it if the waitress finds out how we can contact Willy?"

"More logic. I'm impressed." He tapped the back of her hand with one finger, then sat back, the contact broken. And as the distance between them grew, a vague feeling of isolation flitted through Carin. His face sobered. "What if this Willy doesn't remember seeing Daniel?"

She sat back herself, deliberately building on the distance so she could think clearly. "Then we'll keep going. There's another place just outside of Yuma that I told Daniel about."

"How did you learn about all these places?"

"I told you I got lost and found this place, and I travel this way a lot." She picked up the menu and used it as a plastic barrier between the two of them. "And I like to eat. I'm starved. How about you?"

"Yeah. I'm pretty hungry."

"Good." She scanned the menu. "I'll have the club sandwich and fries." She chanced a look at him over the top of the menu and was startled to find him staring at her intently. "Now you're doing it."

"Doing what?"

"Looking at me as if I was a bug on a display board."

The smile tugged at his lips again. "Not a bug, I assure you. I was just thinking that for being such an expert on food, you look as if a good wind could blow you away."

She felt her face warm and cursed the reaction. "I've got great metabolism," she said, hiding behind the menu again.

Right then the waitress came back, and Carin lowered the menu as the woman put the iced teas on the table. "You're in luck," the woman said. "Willy was on the way here anyway, and it won't take longer than twenty minutes. Do you want to order something while you wait?"

Carin closed the menu and reached for her iced tea. "I'll have the club sandwich on whole wheat, not toasted, extra tomatoes and mayonnaise, fries and a dill pickle, but only if the pickle's kosher. If it's not, forget that and give me some olives, the green kind with pimento stuffing."

"How about you?" Stella asked David.

"A ham and cheese sandwich," David said handing her the menu. "And let us know as soon as Willy gets here."

FIFTEEN MINUTES LATER David knew that he shouldn't have ordered any food. His sandwich sat like a rock in his stomach. He finished the last of his iced tea, laid his napkin over the remainder of his meal and glanced at Carin.

She looked delicate, almost waiflike, yet she'd finished off her meal completely and was scanning the dessert menu displayed on the side of the napkin container.

"Are you still hungry?" he asked.

The navy blue eyes turned on him and for a fraction of a second he felt his breath catch. "I thought some ice cream would be nice." She frowned at his half-eaten sandwich. "Didn't you like it?"

He shook his head. "It was fine. I just didn't have much of an appetite." He glanced at the door, but didn't see anyone coming in. "I wish Willy would get here so we could get on with things."

"Since we have to wait a bit longer, I think I'm going to have a banana split with chocolate, vanilla, and strawberry ice cream with chocolate, pineapple and caramel syrup topped with whipped cream and a maraschino cherry."

He looked back at her, startled to find her smiling at him, her eyes crinkled with humor. "Are you really—"

"Just kidding. I was just seeing if you were listening," she murmured. "Actually, I don't eat maraschino cherries. They never decompose. They put a maraschino cherry in a compost pile and it was still there a year later."

He wondered if this woman was ever predictable. "Where did you hear that?"

"I don't remember, but I filed it away and have since avoided maraschino cherries. What I'd like is a small dish of vanilla ice cream."

David looked up to try to catch Stella's eye to get Carin her ice cream, but saw she was near the front door, deep in conversation with a tiny, elderly woman dressed in an oversize white T-shirt and white baggy pants that hung on her rail-thin frame. She frowned up at Stella as the waitress spoke, then the tiny woman looked at David's table. With a nod to Stella, the woman made her way across the restaurant in their direction.

She approached the booth and David found himself being studied by faded blue eyes set in a heavily lined face. At first her gaze through the smoke from a cigarette she had caught at the side of her mouth was narrowed and assessing, but as she got closer, her eyes widened. The cigarette bobbed up and down as the woman said, "Hot damn, honey, you came back to see Willy just like you promised!"

Chapter Five

David stared at her. "Willy?"

"Of course, it's me." She tapped her frail chest with a hand knotted from arthritis. "You still going to use me in one of them books of yours?"

He didn't realize until then that he never really thought they'd find anyone who had met Daniel. But they'd struck gold and it gave him a rush of excitement. "You know me?"

"I never forget a promise." She smiled and arched a thin brow that had been penciled on her pale skin. "Or a handsome face, lover." As the smoke curled upward, a long ash hung precariously from the end of the cigarette. "You know, you look different." She moved closer and took the cigarette out of her mouth. "Yeah, you cleaned up a bit, cut your hair, and you're wearing different clothes...." She glanced at Carin, then back to David. "And you were alone before. Don't tell me you're married after all?"

Willy was exactly the kind of character that Daniel would have had a field day with. "No. I'm not married."

"Thank the saints." Abruptly, she dropped down on the seat by Carin, scooting over and forcing Carin to get closer to the corner of the booth. Then she sat forward, leaning across the table to talk to David. "So, tell me, lover, did I make it into that book of yours?"

Carin was pressed into the corner of the booth and was as inconspicuously as possible trying to wave away the smoke. "This is Dr. Carin Walker," David said to include Carin in the conversation, but Willy didn't even spare Carin another look.

"So, you brought your own doc along with you this time, eh?"

"Willy, I have to explain something to you," David said, sitting forward.

"Explain away, lover," she said as she grabbed the ashtray by the dessert card and flicked her ashes in it. Then she rested her elbows on the table. "I'm all ears."

"I'm not who you think I am."

She took a drag on the cigarette, then squinted at him through the trickle of exhaled smoke. "Then who are you, Peter Rabbit?"

David took out the pictures and laid them in front of her on the table. "That's Daniel, my twin."

She squinted at the pictures, picked up the PR shot, then looked at David over it. "These aren't you?"

"No."

"Get outta here."

"I'm serious. I've never been in here before. You met my brother."

Carin waved faintly at the haze of smoke that was circling in the air and coughed softly before she asked, "When was Daniel in here?"

"Daniel? He said his name was T. J."

"He goes by that name sometimes," David said quickly.

Willy flicked the ashes in the ashtray again and finally acknowledged Carin's existence with a slanted glance from her faded eyes. "You're really a doc?"

"Yes, and the man you met is really his twin."

"Get outta here," she muttered and looked back to David. "Damn, you had me fooled, lover. If you aren't him, then what did you need to see me for in such a hurry?"

"Willy, I'm looking for my brother."

"Is he in trouble?" she asked.

"I don't know. I hope not."

"Then what's going on?"

"Daniel left for a research trip, and he was supposed to be back a week ago. No one's seen him or heard from him since he took off on the trip. He left over a month ago."

"Damn." She took a pack of cigarettes out of her shirt pocket and took her time lighting another cigarette off the one that was burned to the filter. As she crushed the first one in the ashtray, she looked at David. "What do you want from me?"

A miracle, he thought, but he said, "He didn't happen to give you a hint about where he was going from here, did he?"

"Sure, I know where he went."

Was this his miracle? "You do?" David asked.

"Sure. He was having trouble with his bike, something to do with the brakes, and I told him to go see Crazy Rick."

"Who?"

"Rick Schwartz. I've called him Crazy Rick for as long as I can remember. He's a bit off, but he's the local expert on Harleys. They're sort of like an obsession with him. He's got some real old ones, and if anyone'd know what's wrong with the one your brother had, Crazy Rick's the man to see. Told your brother all about him. Figured he'd gone there when he left here."

"Where's Rick's place?"

"Go toward Blakeney and take the Antelope Road turnoff. Go about four miles until you come to a pasture on the right where they're grazing sheep. Take a right and Crazy Rick's place is about two miles down that road."

"I take it he doesn't have a shop?"

"Naw, he's got a bunch of land with a mobile on it and a whole slew of old bikes and some trucks. You can't miss it." She took a drag and exhaled on a hiss. "Hope to hell you make contact." As she stood, she asked, "Is your brother really a big-time writer?"

"He writes the T. J. Pierce novels." She looked blank. "Mystery novels." He moved the closer picture of Daniel to face her. "That's the picture that's on the cover of his books."

She looked down at it, a professional photo, just head and shoulders, the lighting used to accentuate the cut of his cheekbones and his deep eyes. "Well, I'll say one thing."

"What's that?"

She took a long drag on the cigarette, then spoke as she exhaled. "He wasn't handing me a line of bull. You know, most men that come through here, they tell you tall stories, like they're the king of Siam or something. And who's to know?'' She shook her head. "When you find him, tell him to come by and see me when he's back this way again.''

"I'll tell him,'' David said.

As she walked off toward the back of the place, David stood and tossed money on the table. He looked at Carin. "Let's get going.''

"Oh, I exist?'' she said as she slid out of the booth and fumbled in her purse to take out her sunglasses.

She very definitely existed, he thought. "Willy's a character, isn't she?''

"Hot damn, you know she is, lover,'' Carin muttered as she flashed David a smile, slipped on her sunglasses and went past him to head to the door.

As he watched her walk away, the world suddenly narrowed to her, to the way she moved, the contrast of the hot-pink of her top with the golden tone of her skin, and the white shorts that did little to hide the curve of her hips. "Oh, yes, you exist, Doctor,'' he murmured and followed her to the door.

He was almost thankful for the blanketing heat when he stepped out of the restaurant. It gave him a focus beyond Carin, and it let him think with some clarity. This wasn't the time to be looking at her like that, especially when she could look at him as if she could see into his soul. The idea almost stopped him dead. That was crazy, to think she could see his soul— if he had a soul.

He kept walking, heading for the convertible, yet the thoughts refused to diffuse. He remembered being nine and feeling as if his mother's third husband had X-ray vision, that he could have seen right into his brain if he'd tried.

He stopped by the driver's door of the car and looked at Carin. What combination of being around this woman, having Daniel missing, and the nightmares, had produced that memory? He hadn't thought about the man for years and now he was popping up all over the place. But he had no answers to his own question. Instead, he held out his hand for her keys. "Is it all right if I drive?"

"Sure." As she dropped the keys in his hand, she looked at him. "Is something wrong?"

He had an urge to tell her, to explain what had just happened, but stopped that thought before it fully formed. There was no way he was going to tell a psychologist any of that. "No, why?"

"I thought you'd be thrilled that Willy not only remembered Daniel, but she knew where he went."

"I am. I'm just anxious to get to Crazy Rick's place."

"Then let's get going." She went around the car to get in. When David slipped in behind the wheel and she settled in the passenger seat, she asked, "Do you want to put up the top?"

"Later." He started the car, and headed toward the freeway.

When Carin laughed he was startled. "What's so funny?"

"I was just thinking how strange this all sounds. We're going to find someone called Crazy Rick because a little gnome of a woman called Willy told us to. Crazy Rick and Willy sounds like the name of a movie, like *Molly and Lawless John*."

He glanced at her, the wind catching at her hair as she fought to get it back under her cap. "Molly and who?"

"It's an old movie with Vera Miles and Sam Elliot in it. You never saw it?"

"No."

"Get outta here," she said, mimicking Willy perfectly.

And it was his turn to laugh, something he hadn't done for a very long time. "A perfect Willy," he said.

"What a character. She's got to be seventy if she's a day, and she's coming on to a man half her age. It's sort of like Gloria Swanson in *Sunset Boulevard* with William Holden."

"You're a regular encyclopedia of movies, aren't you?"

"A veritable expert on trivia of all sorts."

"The maraschino cherry thing?"

"Exactly. I know lots of information, but none of it makes a bit of difference in the scheme of life." He felt her shift in the seat and he knew she was looking at him, but he didn't take his eyes off the road ahead as they approached the on-ramp. "Did you think we'd ever find anyone who remembered Daniel?"

"No," he said honestly and swung onto the freeway heading east. He sank back in the bucket seat and wished he'd taken the time to put up the top. The sun was beyond hot, almost to a level where the heat was gone and replaced by an intensity that couldn't even be described.

As if Carin had read his mind, she flipped on the air conditioner and turned it on high. "Is that better?" she asked as she adjusted the vents that blew on him.

"Air-conditioning in a convertible?" he said. "What a concept."

"It works," she said as she fiddled with the vents until cool air was rushing over his arms and against his chest. "You get the cold air blowing on your face and you feel cooler all over."

"Mind over matter?"

"Sort of. Ron used to say that if you gave the body enough positive signals, you could fool it into thinking what you wanted it to think."

"Who's Ron?"

"An ex-fiancé."

"I thought your ex-fiancé's name was Hank the detective?"

"Hank was my last fiancé. Ron was my first fiancé."

He looked at her, shocked by her calm statement. "Your what?"

"I was engaged to Ron for a while, about three months."

"What happened to poor Ron?"

"Poor Ron?" He could see the way her eyebrows rose, despite being partially hidden behind the large sunglasses. "He wasn't even close to poor," she said.

"Why didn't you marry him?"

"I couldn't."

"Would it bother you if I asked you why you couldn't?"

"No, of course not. I asked myself that a lot of times, but it all boiled down to the fact that he was pretty possessive and he resented my family."

"And you didn't know that before you agreed to marry him?"

"I probably knew it, but I didn't really face it for a while. Maybe that's why I insisted on a long engagement. My sister said that she thought I was doing what I thought was right, but knew deep down that it wasn't."

"Is your sister a shrink?"

"No, she's a pediatrician and painfully honest."

"And you're not?"

"I'm honest. I don't have a good enough memory to tell lies. But I tend to hedge my bets."

"Hedging your bets? It sounds more like marriage is another phobia of yours."

"That's enough. I agreed not to psychoanalyze you, so don't do it to me. Besides, I've been engaged, but Daniel said you haven't even come close."

Damn Daniel. It was bad enough that he was baring his soul to this woman. David didn't want his life laid out on display for her, too. "Are we matching weakness for weakness?"

"No, of course not. I was just making a point."

"What point?"

"You don't even let people get close, so marriage would have never been a possibility."

This woman sure knew which buttons to push. "How in the hell would you know that?" he barked.

As if she had no clue that he was furious, she calmly ticked off reasons. "You're thirty-eight years old and you live alone in a rented apartment, and the idea of being close to anyone, even your own twin brother, is, at best, uncomfortable for you."

His anger grew with each word she uttered. "I live in an apartment because I don't have time for a house, and I'm as close to Daniel as you probably are to any

of your siblings. And the idea of being close to anyone is not uncomfortable for me. But—" he flashed
her a direct glare "—I haven't been engaged twice and
changed my mind because I made stupid mistakes."

"I saved myself *before* I made stupid mistakes," she
countered. "There's a difference."

"Oh, really?" he muttered.

"Absolutely. I took the chance. You never did."

"You told me that I don't know you. Well, you
don't know me either, Doctor."

She didn't say anything else, and David was inordinately thankful. She shifted in her seat, reached for
her briefcase in the back, then drew it up onto her lap.
While she sorted through it, he spotted the sign for
Antelope Road.

He exited, then headed the way Willy had told him
to go. A quick glance at Carin told him she was busy
writing in the three-ring binder she'd laid on top of her
closed briefcase. Let her write, as long as she didn't
keep baiting him.

It was true he'd never considered marriage with any
of the women who had come in and out of his life. In
fact, at that moment, he couldn't even really remember any one woman he'd been very close to. He drove
down the road that cut through the barren land to the
south, and he was taken aback when Carin spoke.

"I suppose I should apologize to you."

"Damn straight you should," he muttered and
pulled off the road onto the shoulder. As the car idled,
he turned in the leather seat and gripped the headrest
of her seat. "Are you going to admit you've made too
many unattractive assumptions about me?"

She slipped off her glasses and her eyes widened. "No, I'm just—"

Impulsiveness had never been a part of his life, but he'd be damned if he'd let this woman dissect him when she didn't know anything about him. Before his thought process caught up with his action, he had reached out to take her by her shoulders, and despite the console that separated the two seats, he pulled her to him. He had a flashing glimpse of her eyes filled with shock just before he pressed his lips to hers.

He wanted to linger, to taste every bit of her, but he barely had the taste of her on his tongue when he stopped and held her at arm's length. He tempered his anger with the satisfaction that he'd truly shocked her.

"Don't tell me I can't get close to another person," he cautioned and turned from the sight of her, killing a sudden need to touch her gently and feel her under his hands. "Just because you know Daniel, that doesn't make you an expert on me. And for the short time we're in this car together, do me a favor and drop the doctor act. This isn't your office, and I'm not with you to be analyzed."

He gripped the steering wheel and spun the tires getting back onto the road.

The silence was electric until he felt Carin shift and when she spoke, her voice was low, but even. "You're right. Absolutely."

He darted her a look, but her glasses were back in place and her hands were pressed flat to the book she'd been writing in. "No more doctor act. No more analyzing," she said. "Just two people looking for another person."

If she'd tried to take the wind out of his sails, she couldn't have done a better job of it. Or she couldn't have made him feel more foolish. And that only angered him more. But he didn't have a clue what to say, so he choked back the anger that refused to go away and muttered, "Good."

Carin sat back in the seat, swallowing repeatedly and pressing her hands to her notebook to keep from touching her lips. She hadn't expected such a literal rebutting of her theory. And she hadn't expected to feel as if she had been blindsided by a force so great that it left her stunned.

She stared ahead at the barren land all around, and took even breaths. She hated herself for arguing with David, and for telling him about her past. She seldom talked about that with anyone, let alone a man who saw her as some voodoo worker who was trying to peer into his brain. And she hated the fact that when he'd kissed her, she had felt instant regret that it was to prove a point rather than to satisfy a genuine urge.

Get a grip, she told herself as she glanced at David. His knuckles were white from clenching the wheel, and she had a horrible mental image of him with those fingers around her throat. That's probably what he'd originally had in mind back there.

He'd shaken her, but she'd definitely hit a nerve with him. The man was the traditional loner despite being a twin. And he had no idea that he purposefully isolated himself. She settled in the seat and closed her notebook, fascinated at an insight that had come to her in his burst of anger.

Daniel was a people person, yet he held most people at arm's length, taking them on his own terms.

And David had given new meaning to the word, contained, until moments ago. She looked at him. Attractive, intelligent, and so self-contained that it made her teeth ache.

"Sheep."

She jumped, startled out of her thoughts. "What?"

He motioned ahead of them, and she saw what he was talking about. What looked like thousands of sheep were grazing in a sunburned field to the right, their dirty gray color almost blending in with the browns of the weeds and scrub grass.

He turned onto a dirt road just after the field and as dust rose behind the convertible, Carin wanted to break the tension between them. She hated the feeling that he was just waiting for her to say something he could jump on. It bothered her that this hazel-eyed man didn't see anything valid in what she was doing, but she didn't know what to say to make things better.

As the BMW crested a low hill, Carin looked ahead and knew they'd found Crazy Rick. Less than a hundred yards down the road, behind a six-foot-high fence fashioned of multiple strands of rusted barbed wire, was a single wide mobile home in red, white and blue stripes, and surrounded by the carcasses of old cars, trucks and motorcycles.

David slowed the car as they approached a double chain-link gate. On the wire mesh hung a hand-lettered sign: If You Ever Want Me To Consider Working On Your Bike, Don't Park In Front Of My Gate.

"Welcome to Crazy Rick's," David murmured and stopped the car just beyond the gates.

Before Carin could get out, David was out and heading toward the gate. She hurried up to him as he reached for a rope attached to a cowbell that hung from the gatepost inside the gates. He tugged on the rope and the peal of the bell reverberated in the hot air.

Before the sound died off in the shimmering heat, two huge Dobermans came charging around the side of the mobile, making their way through the junk, barking and snarling. They headed straight for the gates. As they hurled themselves at the chain-link barrier, Carin felt David grab her by the arm and jerk her back a good two feet.

Carin steadied herself by grabbing hold of the hand with which David held her, and stared at the dogs snarling and barking behind the gate. "Willy never said anything about the man having killer dogs."

David didn't move, but he yelled over the barking, "Hey, Rick! Rick!"

Carin looked past the dogs to the patriotic-looking mobile home, covered with rust spots and what looked like American flags hanging in the windows. When one of the curtains shifted slightly, she moved closer to David. "He's in there. He's looking at us from the front window on the right."

"He's not coming out."

"Maybe he's just trying to figure out if we're here to make trouble for him."

"I didn't park in front of his damn gate," David muttered. "What more does he want?"

"He's obviously an eccentric."

"That's being polite."

"He needs reassurance."

"All right, Dr. Walker, in your professional opinion, just what's the best way to handle this? Knock out the dogs and sprint for the trailer? Or do we just stand here baking in the sun and he'll come out to take care of our carcasses when we're dead?"

"Just stand here. Let him get a good look until he's satisfied. Who knows, maybe he'll be like Willy, think you're Daniel and let down his guard? At least we're safe out here for now."

He slanted a raised eyebrow in her direction, then glanced down at her hand still tightly holding his. "Are we?"

Quickly she drew her hand back, but stayed close to David while she stared at the dogs. "Maybe we should go back to Willy's and ask her how to handle this."

"Not on your life. I've come this far, I'm going to see Rick." He cupped his hands at his mouth. "Rick! Rick! Are you in there?"

Nothing happened.

"Rick? Are you in there?"

Suddenly a long, high-pitched whistle cut through the air, and miraculously, the animals stopped barking. Without taking their eyes off David and Carin, they sank to their haunches inches from the gate. The door to the trailer opened and they watched a man come out onto the rickety wooden porch.

In tie-dye T-shirt with the sleeves ripped out, cutoff jeans that exposed bowed legs, and matted hair held back from a lined face with a leather headband, the man gripped a narrow porch support and stared at the gate. A double-barreled shotgun rested in the crook of his arm.

Crazy Rick. David had no doubt who the man was.

"He's got a gun," Carin breathed and David felt her move even closer to him, pressing the heat of her arm against his.

"It's a shotgun, and I guess Willy didn't think it was important to tell us the man's dangerous," he said in a low voice. "Any ideas on how to handle this?"

"We can run for it," she whispered.

"I was hoping you'd have some psychology that would work on him."

"I don't think he's in the mood to talk."

David tensed as Crazy Rick jumped off the porch and started for the gates. The dogs never moved, but their low growls didn't stop. David waited until the bowlegged man was right behind the dogs, then he spoke up. "We're looking for Rick."

The man squinted at Carin, but didn't say a thing.

"Willy sent us to talk to him," David said quickly.

The man pushed between the dogs, the shotgun still over his arm. When he spoke, he spoke to Carin. "How'd you know Willy?" he asked, his voice like well used gravel.

"We were at her place, and she said you might be able to give us some information," Carin said.

"Like what?"

"This man's brother was at Willy's place around the end of June. She said she sent him out here."

"Why'd she do a thing like that?"

David felt sweat trickling from his hair down his temples, and his shirt stuck to his skin. "He had trouble with his bike," he said. "She told us you were an expert on old Harleys."

Rick didn't even glance at David. "Yeah, so what?" he asked Carin.

She shifted closer to David, her arm pressing against his. David wanted to wipe at the moisture on his face, but he didn't want to make any quick moves. "He was having trouble with the brakes on his motorcycle," he said.

Rick acted as if David was invisible, as if the words he said had less impact than a drop of water in the ocean, and it was making David nervous. Just about as nervous as he felt when the man stroked the gun over his arm. "What'd he have?" Rick asked Carin.

Carin nudged David. "I forgot what he had," she whispered.

"A '55 Harley, modified."

"A 1955 Harley-Davidson, modified."

"You know anything about bikes, sister?"

David glanced at Carin who shook her head. "Not much."

"Well, if you knew diddly about them, you'd know that that bike is one righteous machine."

"My brother *was* here?" David asked.

Rick kept talking right over David's question. "Soon as it rolled in here, I said to myself, that's one cherry creation, Ricky boy."

"He was here?" Carin asked.

"Yeah, he come by a while back. Had a bad setup on his brakes."

Anxious to find out everything he could, David started toward the gate, but stopped after one step when the dogs stood and Rick raised the muzzle of the shotgun to point it right at David's chest.

Chapter Six

"Sister, tell that person to stay right where he is," Rick said venomously.

David stared at the man. Carin whispered to him, "Willy said he was crazy. Don't move." Then she said to Rick, "He won't come any closer. I give you my word."

"Bob, Jerry, enough," Rick said as the shotgun lowered and the dogs backed off. When he waved a hand at the animals, they turned and loped off toward the mobile home. They flopped down in the sparse shade of an old Ford truck, but never took their eyes off David.

Rick stood absolutely still for what seemed like forever, then he propped the shotgun against the barbed wire and unlocked the gate. It squeaked loudly when he pulled it open and stepped through. Without a glance at David, he went directly to Carin.

"Take 'em off," he said abruptly as he stopped a few feet from her.

"Excuse me?" Carin asked as David clenched his hands into fists. He could see the color rising in her face, color that didn't come from the flush of heat.

"The shades. I need to see your eyes. Take 'em off."

She slipped off her sunglasses and looked right at Rick, her eyes narrowed from the brilliance of the desert sun. "How's this?"

He exhaled. "Better. Now, what's all this to you?"

"We're looking for the man on the bike," she said.

Rick was about five foot six or so. If he had chosen to acknowledge David's existence, he would have had to look up a good five inches to make eye contact. Even though Rick was staring only at Carin, David could see his eyes were puffy and bloodshot. "Why're you looking for him?"

David inhaled and almost choked on the smell of unwashed body and a sickening sweetness. He didn't have to inhale again to know why the man's eyes looked like they did. Obviously Crazy Rick had some help getting crazy. "He was supposed to be home a week ago, but he hasn't shown up yet."

"The man was cruising. No need to be nowhere. Got his bike between his legs, the wind at his back. No need to be nowhere." He smiled at Carin and showed discolored, uneven teeth. "You'd look great on a bike, sister."

Even though Carin was still blushing, David had to admit that she had a touch with people. She gave a casual, "Thanks," then got right to the point. "Where did he say he was going when he left here?"

He squinted as he rocked forward toward Carin. "His bike was teetering when he showed up. He was worried about it. But Rick got it going real good. Got to tell you, that bike is cherry. Hope nothing happened to it."

"That's what we're trying to figure out, what happened to the bike and his twin brother."

Rick shook his head. "Naw, no way."

"Yes, we're looking—"

"They're not twins. Nope. No way. That's a lie. I hate lies."

"No, I swear it's the truth."

"The aura's all wrong."

"Whose aura?" Carin asked intently.

Rick motioned toward David with his head, making his matted hair swing crazily around his shoulders. It was the closest he'd come to actually acknowledging David's presence. "His brother had a great aura, lots of blue in it, a bit of green. A hell of a good one." He never took his eyes off Carin. "Red's bad. Saw it the second this one came. Don't like it, not one bit." He backed up a half-pace, and as David took a relatively fresh breath, Rick muttered, "It's trouble. Auras don't lie."

David's immediate impulse was to shake the information out of the lunatic, then get the hell out of there, but that obviously wasn't Carin's impulse. She actually moved forward, toward Rick, meeting him almost toe-to-toe. "You read auras, don't you?" she asked in an almost confidential voice.

"Yeah, have since..." he closed his eyes, then slowly opened them "...'67. The summer of '67. Right after a Grateful Dead concert. The vibrations were awesome then. Suddenly I saw auras on everyone. A miracle, I called it. A gift. I don't see many who radiate what his brother did. Awesome, sister, totally awesome. But this one here... his aura's trouble, real radical trouble... heavy."

David was hot and miserable and felt as invisible as a speck of lint. Worse yet, he was sure the man was going to use the word groovy at any minute. "Rick, listen. My brother—"

The man spoke right over David. "Hey, you want to come in and commune for a while, sister? I got some incense that'll blow your mind."

"I'd love to if I had the time, but tell me why this man's aura is so troubled."

He turned a shoulder to David and spoke in a low voice to Carin. "Do you really want to know, sister?"

"Yes, please."

As the heat beat down all around, Rick closed his eyes, threw his head back, held his arms straight out at his sides and yelled to the heavens, "Aaahh."

David didn't have a doubt in the world that the man was certifiable and probably couldn't tell them anything about Daniel. He looked at Carin, ready to give her the high sign to get out of there, but she wasn't looking at him. She was holding onto her sunglasses with both hands and watching Rick intently.

"Rick?" she said softly. "Rick?"

The echo of his voice trailed off in the hot desert air as his arms lowered and his eyes opened. "It's heavy, heavy."

Carin didn't give a clue if she was getting impatient with his ramblings. "What's heavy?" she asked.

"I gotta get back inside. Don't like being out here around this one. Bad enough he's here, but..."

"Can't you just talk to him and tell him about his brother?" she asked.

He shook his head, his matted hair looping back and forth on his shoulders. "Can't talk to him. Can't do it."

David felt gooseflesh on his skin, even though the heat had to be over one hundred degrees.

"All right, that's fair." Carin moved a bit closer. "Just tell me around *when* his brother came through here, you fixed his Harley, and he left."

"Right on, sister."

"How long was he here?"

"Don't know. Time's a lie."

"All right," Carin said, obviously regrouping. "Was he here overnight?"

"No." Rick began to rock back and forth slowly. "All I had to do on the bike was fix the brake line. He took off before sunset."

"He went east?"

"Yeah, east. He was going to camp out. No motels for him. No wooden boxes, just the stars and moon."

"Did he say where he was going to camp?"

"There's a lot of land east of here, past Yuma."

David watched Carin looking at Rick in her intent way. The bill of her cap shaded her face partially, but he could see the film of perspiration on her skin from the unrelenting sun.

"Rick, you know this country like the back of your hand, don't you?"

"You bet, sister."

"And if you were camping out that way, where would you camp?"

David watched Carin working subtly with this man, getting exactly what they needed to know. "He asked me the same thing, the same thing."

"And what did you tell him, Rick?" Carin prodded.

"Told him I'd go to the only place any righteous biker would go. The place of power."

David didn't move as Carin asked, "What's the power?"

"The universal power, the single thought, mind, action." He closed his eyes and rocked again. "Touch it. Feel it. Become it."

"Rick, where's the place of power?" she persisted.

He leaned toward her and spoke in a voice that was just above a whisper. "Hell's Way, sister, Hell's Way."

David stared at the man. Hell's Way. Carin had done it, and done it with real finesse.

"Can you tell me how to find Hell's Way?" she asked, lowering her voice to match the man's tone.

Rick glanced back over his shoulder, not exactly looking at David, but enough to make sure David wasn't too close. Then he turned, went even closer to Carin and all David heard was mumbling. When he drew back, he put two fingers to his mouth, let out a low piercing whistle, and the dogs came running.

The huge animals kicked up dust as they headed out the gate, and as David braced himself, the dogs went to Rick and flanked him. "Peace, sister," Rick said, holding up two fingers. He turned without a glance at David and headed for the gates, the dogs in step at his side. He stopped just long enough to close and lock the gate again, then he headed back to the mobile home.

When the man disappeared with the dogs into the red, white and blue trailer, David exhaled with relief and turned to Carin. He was taken aback to see her staring after Rick, her face stamped with a look of understanding that made his heart lurch. She understood this man and his jibberish in a way David couldn't.

He hated his feeling of helplessness. And he hated it even more that his first impulse was to reach out to Carin, to pull her to him and ward off those feelings. He ran both hands roughly over the dampness of his face. The fact that the impulse remained, even after the kiss, disturbed him greatly.

Carin slipped on her sunglasses, hiding her eyes, and when she turned to head for the car, he fell in step beside her. He sought something to break his strange mood. "So, do I exist?" he asked as they neared the car.

Carin glanced at him as she opened the passenger door, her eyes shaded. "Rick's sort of like a male Willy," she said, but no hint of humor touched her face. "Don't you think?"

"Yeah, with a bad hairdo," he said as he went around to the driver's side. Carin was pushing the back of her seat to the upright position while he slipped in behind the wheel. When he touched his seat, he felt as if he'd been burned, even through the material of his jeans.

"Whoa," he breathed as he gingerly eased himself onto the scorching leather seat.

Carin closed her door. "The first lesson you learn when you get a convertible is to always, always tip the back of the seat forward when you get out so it shades the bottom part."

"Is there anything else about a convertible you forgot to tell me?" he asked as he turned on the motor.

"Know when it's time to put up the top, and now's the time."

"Just tell me what to do," David said, the heat so oppressive that it had almost become a state of mind, similar in its intensity to the way he felt around this woman.

Carin took care of the top cover, then as the power top eased up and over the passenger space, she instructed David how to fasten it to the frame. The shade immediately diminished the heat, and as David snapped the lever into place, Carin adjusted the air-conditioner.

Cool waves of air not only blew over his skin, they began to fill the air around him. As the windows slid up, the coolness felt as refreshing as a drink of water. Yet as good as it felt, he had to admit that it made the space he shared with Carin shrink to the point that he could swear her delicate scent filled every molecule.

Carin sank back in the seat with a sigh. "How's that?"

"Better," he murmured, but jumped when he touched the steering wheel.

"What do you do about the steering wheel in a convertible?" he asked as he adjusted an air-conditioning duct to blow toward the wheel.

"You keep a towel under the seat to throw over it. I should have thought of that."

"Is there anything else I should know?" he asked expectantly as he slipped the car into gear and turned on the dirt road to head back toward the freeway.

"Not that I can think of."

"Don't you think you should tell me where we're going?"

"Oh. East toward Yuma. That was strange what Rick was saying about your aura, wasn't it?"

Her words caught at David. "Do you believe in auras?"

"No."

That denial shocked him. "You acted as if every word Rick said was completely valid."

"It didn't matter what I believed or didn't believe. What's important is the fact that Rick believed it, and he was the one who had the information we needed."

"I think a good dose of hallucinogenics gave him his so-called gift."

"That, mixed with a fair amount of pot."

He glanced at her as she settled back in the seat. "You could tell?"

"Only when I breathed."

"Do you think he told you the truth?"

"Sure."

"How can you be so sure?"

"He said I have an aura of peace, that he only trusted people who had that aura. He trusted me. He wouldn't even look at you."

David had the thought that maybe the man only trusted beauty, but he knew that wasn't the truth about Crazy Rick. "The man's a lunatic," he muttered.

That brought Carin up straight, and he knew she was glaring at him even if he wasn't looking at her. "He's not a lunatic," she said tightly. "I hate that word."

"I just meant—"

"He's just living in his own world. He made it so he can survive. That doesn't make him a lunatic. Maybe paranoid, and maybe out of touch with reality, but he's no lunatic.''

"Sorry for my choice of words. I guess you wouldn't call any of your patients lunatics.''

"I don't have patients, but if I did, I certainly wouldn't label them.''

He looked at her as she slipped lower in the seat, drew her legs up to her chest with her heels on the edge of the seat and wrapped her arms around her slender legs. "What do you mean you don't have patients? You're a doctor.''

She nibbled on her bottom lip. "But I don't have a practice. I'm in research.''

And that's too bad, he thought. Here she was chasing some crazy idea about mental links, but just seeing her deal with Rick showed him she had her own gift, dealing with damaged people. "Why don't you go back to a practice?''

"There's nothing to go back to. I've never practiced. I went right from my internship to the research.''

"Are you ever going to practice?''

She was silent for a very long time, and just before they came to the on-ramp, she finally said, "I always thought I would, but I'm not sure.''

"About what?''

"Dealing with people. There's so much pain in people, and so much need, and it's a never-ending need.''

He swung onto the freeway and sped up as he headed east to Yuma. "Are you hedging your bets by staying in research for now?''

He was certain she'd jump all over him, but she didn't. He heard her exhale softly, then speak in a low voice. "That's a possibility."

He didn't want to feel as if he'd just broken through a layer of Dr. Walker's emotional armor, but he knew he had. "You dealt with Rick easily enough."

"It was hard, believe me. The man's damaged beyond belief, but he's no lunatic." She shifted in the seat, and David could feel her looking at him. "Your brother finds the strangest people, doesn't he?"

David knew she was changing the subject and he didn't fight it. "He always has. He draws them the way my mother draws strange husbands." Carin laughed at that, and David was shocked that there was no residual sarcasm behind his own statement. That was a first for him. Maybe the good doctor was more effective with people than even he thought. "Speaking of my brother, when are you going to tell me what Rick told you?"

"He said to go east. Go past Yuma."

"And?"

As the coolness of the air conditioner trailed over her skin, Carin shivered slightly, but she knew it wasn't because of the cold air. It came from remembering Rick whispering that he was afraid to make eye contact with David in case he died from it. The words of a paranoid man, or the product of one too many joints, or one too many trips?

She'd seen psychosis up close, but she couldn't forget the look in Rick's eyes. "You got this aura, real strong, but he don't," he'd hissed at her in the blanketing heat. "He's broken. His aura's a nightmare. Find Hell's Way. Find it and make things right."

"Make what things right?" she'd asked.

"When he came up, I knew. It's the dying. It's gotta be made right or it's going to come. It's coming down big-time."

"What dying?"

"The dying," he'd muttered intently, as if he was angered that she had to ask. "You know."

She'd known that there was no way to get him to explain, so she'd asked, "Where can I find Hell's Way?"

Rick had come even closer, the sickly sweet smell of marijuana clinging to him so strong that it had almost choked her. "You gotta get past Yuma. Go to the peaks, the touching ones. The power's there. The bonding, coming together. Get under it and make it right."

"What peaks?"

He'd narrowed his eyes even more. "This one'll know when he's there. He'll know."

"David will?"

He hadn't looked at David, but he'd rolled his eyes back in his direction. "This one. He'll know."

"How?" she'd persisted.

"His brother knew. This one'll know, too. He has to, or there'll be the dying."

She'd stared at Rick. Did he sense some sort of connection between Daniel and David? "His brother, what happened to him?"

"He found Hell's Way. You find it too...soon."

His eyes had glazed over, and Carin had known right then that Rick had no more to tell. "Thank you, Rick."

He'd moved back, then he'd made the peace sign, called the dogs and went back into his own safe world behind the barbed wire.

"Carin?"

She'd been so lost in thought that it startled her when David said her name. "Yes?"

"Are you going to tell me exactly what Rick said back there?"

David thought she had directions, and Rick thought David was tied to death. Her stomach knotted. She hoped that Rick had no "gift," and that he was only lost in a drugged fog. She wasn't at all sure there even was a place called Hell's Way. She nibbled on her bottom lip. "We have to go past Yuma." she said. "Go until we find the peaks."

He sped up on the almost deserted freeway. "The peaks? What peaks?"

"The peaks that meet, that's all he said. There's power there in the bonding, that you have to go under it. He . . . he said that Daniel found it, that you could find them, too."

"Let me get this straight. He didn't tell you where Hell's Way is, did he?"

"Not exactly, but he said that—"

"How the hell am I supposed to know when these peaks appear?"

"He just said you'd know when you found them. I know it sounds incredible. But he believes that if Daniel found them, so can you."

He slanted her a look that all but told her he thought she was crazy, too. "That dovetails nicely with your ideas, doesn't it?"

She couldn't deny that. "It's something to think about."

"It's ridiculous," he muttered.

Carin sank back in the seat and stared ahead at the shimmering desert. "What do you want to do?"

"If I had half a brain, I'd get out in Yuma and go back to San Diego."

"What are you *going* to do?" she managed to ask.

He flexed his hands on the steering wheel. "Go past Yuma, look for the peaks and Hell's Way."

"And if we don't find them?"

"Then I'll get out at the first town and go back to San Diego to wait for Daniel to contact me."

"Maybe you'll find them."

He slowed a bit and looked at her. "And maybe we'll get caught in a snowstorm."

"But if you found them, then . . ."

"If I found them, we'll be the recipients of more luck than we deserve."

At least he'd be here until they passed Yuma. Looking into his narrowed hazel eyes, she could admit that she wanted him here with her. All the trips she'd taken this way alone had just been something she'd had to do. But this time she knew she didn't want to go this way alone.

"Whatever it is, I hope we find them," she murmured and looked away from David to a sign they were passing. Yuma 75 miles.

LATE IN THE AFTERNOON, David pulled off the freeway and stopped at a tiny gas station that consisted of two pumps and a run-down wooden building displaying a faded Coke sign on the roof along with the declaration, Last Stop Station.

"I'm going to call. Do you want something cold to drink?" David asked as he opened his door.

"Sure. A soda sounds great," Carin said.

David got out, talked to an attendant who began to pump gas, then disappeared into the tiny building.

They had stopped for food at a drive-through in Yuma over two hours ago, and since then, David hadn't spoken more than ten words. He'd kept driving, lost in his own thoughts, and the silence had weighed heavily on Carin.

She looked out the car window. They were in a strange land now, with patches of flat desert that had soaring buttes and mesas exploding off the desert floor. Off in the distance, a tinge of purple hung in the late-afternoon sky. This was the first gas station they'd seen in twenty miles.

The land around here looked as if it had been conceived on an artist's canvas, with rich golds and coppers and the setting sun starting to cast deep purple shadows across the land.

Peaks of all sorts were everywhere. But no set of peaks, or any peaks that looked remarkably different from any of the others. She closed her eyes as she tugged off her cap and tossed it onto the backseat. She shook out her hair, then combed it carelessly with her fingers.

As she sank back against the seat, she admitted that David was close to turning back, and then she'd be on the route alone. A sense of aloneness she'd felt after leaving Crazy Rick's was still there. And that didn't make sense. She usually loved her privacy, the isolation where she could think and mentally go over her data.

When David came out of the building carrying two cans of soda, she watched him stride toward the car. When she'd gone to Daniel's, she'd never expected to run into a man who seemed to be in the process of turning her world upside down. Upside down? She touched her lips with the tips of her fingers. "Upside down and sideways," she murmured as she drew her hand down into a fist on her lap.

She watched David circle the car and pay the attendant. She was inordinately aware of the way he moved, of the tone of his skin, the way his hair clung to his temples and neck. And as her tongue touched her lips, she felt regret that all she tasted was a touch of saltiness. No lingering evidence that David had ever kissed her.

She looked away from him. A kiss? Hardly. Just a way of making a point. A way of showing her she was the crazy one, not him. Her nails dug into the palms of her hands as her fists tightened. She'd never claimed to be totally sane. And David Hart seemed to be the man who could prove it.

David got back behind the wheel and turned to Carin to hand her one of the cans. "Did you call?" she asked quietly.

"Yes," he murmured. "Nothing."

She took the can of soda and cradled it in both hands, pressing her palms to the coolness. "You can try again at the next stop."

"I will." He took a sip of his drink. "I've been thinking that there's no way to tell one peak from another around here, and Daniel wouldn't have stayed on the freeway with his bike.''

She was having trouble focusing past her own thoughts. ''What does that all add up to?''

''The guy inside said that there's a two-lane highway that dips south, that runs parallel to the border. It cuts through the Santa Rosa mountains and passes through an Indian reservation before it goes back up to Tucson. It's about a hundred miles of travel, and I figure we could do that before it gets too late.''

''You think Daniel would have taken that route?''

He shrugged. ''I don't know. All I know is, I would if I was Daniel. He hated the rush of the freeway. Maybe he cut off way back there. Maybe he never even got this far.''

''Did you ask the man if he saw Daniel?''

''He didn't recognize him.''

She watched David, but didn't say anything else as she absorbed the fact that he wasn't giving up easily. He was thinking about how Daniel did things. She didn't say a thing to him, but she had a feeling that something was going to happen.

He took a long drink from his can, then started the car. As he swung onto the side road, he headed toward the hills on a two-lane highway. ''If we haven't found anything by dark, we'll go on to Tucson.''

She wouldn't ask what he'd do then. She didn't want to know.

Chapter Seven

They had driven about twenty miles on a road that seemed to conform to the way the buttes rose out of the valley floor. As long shadows of twilight stretched deeper onto the flatlands, purple images on the barren ground, David knew that he was looking for a needle in a haystack.

"Peaks, peaks everywhere," he muttered.

"Excuse me?" Carin said, her voice soft in the confines of the car.

He made a sweeping motion with his hand to the land outside the car. "Peaks. They're everywhere. Which ones are we looking for?"

"Rick just said peaks, as in two, and that you'd know when you saw them."

"I know that one peak looks like another. Didn't he give you any specifics at all?"

"No," she murmured.

He didn't look at her, but the knowledge that she was keeping something from him hit him like a blow to the stomach. It wasn't instinct or even a hunch. He simply knew it and it shook him. "Why aren't you telling me everything he told you?" he heard himself saying before he was even aware the words would be said.

She spoke quickly, the way she had when he'd first met her at the houseboat. "He rambled on and on about auras and Hell's Way and things like that. That's all. I mean, the man isn't dealing with a full dose of sanity. We already agreed on that. And he sees the world in such strange ways. He's damaged. I don't know what did it, or why or how, but he's not going to make perfect sense with anyone. Maybe just with his bikes. Sort of like an autistic savant who can calculate a mathematical formula, but can't tell you how much a candy bar costs."

He let her run out of steam. "Tell me exactly what he said, and let me see if there's any sense in it."

"I told you, he rambled on about strange things."

As surely as he knew she was withholding something from him, he knew that he couldn't drive any farther. He had to stop, to breathe fresh air and be able to think in a rational manner. He spotted a place to pull off the road and swung onto the dusty widening. He stopped the car, but with the motor idling, he turned to Carin.

Fighting the urge to grip her by her shoulders and shake the truth out of her, he settled for gripping the back of her seat. He pressed the leather with his fingers and met her navy blue gaze. "Now, tell me exactly what Rick said, word for word. And don't lie to me. No hedging your bets on this one."

Her eyes slipped from his gaze, and she stared down at her hands clenched in her lap. "I told you—"

He stopped the lie. "No, you didn't. Rick said something to you back there that you don't want to tell

me about. Well, I've got a bulletin for you, Dr.
Walker, you must tell me *everything* he said.'' Then he
voiced a thought that came from nowhere. "Did he
tell you something happened to Daniel?"

Her mouth tightened. "No, nothing like that." She
sank back in the seat, rested her elbow on the armrest
on the door and stared straight ahead.

"Carin, dammit, what's going on?"

"The truth is that he said your aura was broken,
that it was a nightmare. That you need to get to Hell's
Way to make things right."

The word nightmare hit him, but he made himself
sit very still. "Make what right?"

"I asked him, and he said..." She touched her
tongue to her lips. "He...he said something about the
dying. It's gotta be made right or it's going to come,
something like that, that the dying's coming down big-
time."

His grip on the leather was almost painful and his
ability to draw air into his lungs was escaping him.
"What was he talking about?"

"I don't know." She turned her eyes toward him,
and he saw her pain. She was afraid, and, God help
him, he was starting to feel as if he was going over the
edge. "He acted as if I should know all about it."

"Do you?"

"Of course I don't. He was rambling, I told you
that. Then he said to get past Yuma to the peaks and
the power, to go under and find the power, and that
you'd know it when you saw it."

He uttered a shattering oath, then turned from her
to grip the steering wheel. "And how in the hell am I

supposed to know what to go under or what I'll see when I've never *been* in this part of the country?''

"He didn't say. Maybe he didn't know. Maybe this is all some sort of witch-hunt. God, I wish I could give you the magic words you need to hear, but I can't."

He couldn't think straight. He needed air that wasn't filled with the essence of Carin. He needed to think in a rational pattern and try to figure out how in the hell he ever agreed to start on this wild-goose chase. He opened the door, got out and leaned back against the car to stare across the desert into the distance.

There were no sounds in the air, no other cars on the highway, no planes overhead. Just the soft moan of the wind skimming across the desert and over the irregular surface of the towering buttes. Then he felt the car move and he heard Carin get out. The door closed, then he heard the sound of her footsteps crunching on the gravel and dirt as she came around to him.

"David?"

"What?"

Just then lightning streaked across the sky and a muffled rumbling followed. "Heat lightning," she said. "It happens around here."

"What were you going to say?" he asked, closing his eyes as another bolt cut through the sky.

"I didn't tell you all of that because he really was rambling. He's got this idea that if Daniel found Hell's Way, you could." She exhaled on a sigh. "He seemed to know somehow that Daniel had found it, and that if you found Daniel, your aura could be healed or fixed. That if you didn't find him, there would be dying. How could I tell you something like that?''

As he turned to her, the hazy light of the coming evening touched the hollows at her cheeks and throat with delicate shadows. Her loose hair framed her face, and he saw a gentleness in her that startled him. She was looking at him with an expression that was touched with pity, and he hated that. "I can take anything except a lie."

"I didn't lie to you."

Another bolt of lightning flashed around them, the blue-white light making Carin startlingly clear in front of him. "No, you didn't, not technically."

"I didn't in any way."

He felt tired, weary of everything, including trying to figure out this woman and her ways. He turned from her and walked slowly ahead of where the car was parked. Dust kicked up from his shoes where they struck the ground, and he felt a hint of coolness in the light breeze.

"David?" Carin called after him, but he kept walking. He didn't know where he was going, just that he needed distance between himself and Carin for a while.

But that wasn't to be. Carin hurried after him, and he didn't have to look to know she was beside him, doing an occasional skip step to keep up with him. "Where are you going?" she asked in a breathless voice.

He didn't know. So he kept walking without talking.

After a few minutes, Carin touched his arm. Her hand on his skin was the last straw. He stopped and looked down at where she touched him. "What do you want from me?"

"Just talk to me. Let me know what you're thinking about."

He met her gaze and wondered if this was her best doctor's tone and expression. "Well, Doctor, I seem to be on the run with a woman who thinks we can find a needle in a haystack with mental telepathy."

He hated the words as soon as they came out. He hated the way she jerked back from him, and the way her expression tightened. "I didn't force you into this," she said flatly.

But there had been no way to refuse her. "No one's forced me to do anything. I'm an adult, and I've come to the conclusion that I'm not going any farther."

"You're quitting?"

"I'm not quitting, I'm getting smart. I've had enough of the Crazy Ricks and Willys in this world. I'm going to go back to San Diego and if I have to, I'll hire a private detective. I shouldn't have acted on impulse."

"Heaven forbid you should act on impulse," she muttered.

How could this woman infuriate him so completely, yet look so appealing in the soft light of evening? It was driving him nuts, and he thought he really would need a shrink if he was around her much longer. The decision to leave was becoming more and more like a stab at sanity for him. "I'm going to do the rational thing."

"Which is running away?"

He touched her shoulder with one hand, with the idea of making her listen without adding guilt to his decision. But as soon as he touched her, he knew just how costly impulses could be. The feel of her soft skin

under his hands, the scent that clung to her filling his
senses, blotted out all reason, and the next thing he
knew, he was acting on a dangerous impulse.

He reached for her sunglasses with his other hand,
took them off, then moved closer. As he lowered his
head to hers, he caught a glimpse of her eyes, and
there was no shock there. It took him a full heartbeat
to realize that the heat that came to him in a sudden
rush was echoed in her gaze. Her lips were soft and
warm under his, and as his tongue touched her, her
mouth opened in invitation.

In that moment he knew just how dangerous this
woman could be. Even as his mouth moved on hers,
exploring her and tasting her, he knew he was playing
with something far more potent than heat lightning.
It was fire. A fire that stirred in him, threatening to
consume him, and when he felt her move closer to
him, every place she touched him, branded him.

He drew her closer, and he knew he needed something to make things right, to take away the confusion and ache inside him. And when she circled his
neck with her arms and arched against him, her breasts
crushed to his chest, he had the craziest sensation of
having been in an emotional coma for most of his life
until now. And now every nerve, every atom in his
being, was coming to life.

And in that flashing moment, he knew that he
wanted Carin as completely as he'd ever wanted a
woman before. He wanted every part of her, to be with
her and in her and to never leave her. He felt a trembling in her as she strained to him, and his arousal was
instant.

In this barren land, on a deserted road, at the craziest time of his life, he wanted this woman. Then he remembered the way she'd looked at him earlier, the pity in her eyes, and it brought any craziness to a grinding halt. Sanity took its place and David slowly drew back.

With his hands still on her shoulders, he looked down at her. Her chest rose and fell, her breasts straining against the soft cotton of the bright pink tank top. Everything about her screamed a sensuality that came without premeditation on her part.

And he couldn't take it. Not now. Not like this. He let her go, drawing back to press his hands to the side of his thighs. When had his life begun to spin out of control? The moment he sailed into a nightmare? The moment he saw Carin? The moment he knew Daniel was missing?

He didn't know anything anymore. "So much for acting on impulse," he breathed, not surprised by the hoarseness in his voice or the way his nerves seemed to be raw and painful.

When her tongue darted out to touch her parted lips, David turned from the sight. "It's getting late," he muttered.

Lightning crashed overhead and made him start. "What do you want me to do?" she asked in a low, husky voice as he felt her take her sunglasses from his hand.

He closed his eyes and said the rational thing. "Drop me in Tucson at the airport."

When she didn't say anything, he finally turned and found she was halfway back to the car. As she went farther from him, he had to fight the odd feeling that he was deserting her. Daniel was his brother, not hers. Daniel was a subject of hers, not a real person. Let her go on to Albuquerque and he'd go back to where he belonged.

He looked away from Carin when she got to the car and began to put the convertible top down. Thank goodness he wouldn't have to ride in the closed confines of the car with her to Tucson. The knowledge that a kiss like the one he'd just experienced would happen again if he was close to her kept him where he was.

As he turned from the sight of her fastening the protective lock for the top, he found himself looking up a dirt road that was little more than a trail cutting into and through the rocky mass of a low butte. There were no signs nor road markers, and the wind had cleaned any tracks from the silt on the road. But as David moved back from the opening and looked up at the rough rock and scrub, he suddenly knew he'd found Hell's Way.

Set against the sky that was rapidly being stained with reds and purples, the butte was almost separated into two parts to give access to the land beyond. The sides were rough and weathered and stubbornly, as if refusing to let go of each other, each side shot upward, then inward, toward the middle. They formed a rough arch over the trail.

Peaks, maybe, if he narrowed his eyes to look at the formation, but most certainly something that he could go under. God knew what a man like Rick would see. All David knew was that he was certain he'd found the opening to Hell's Way. He had no doubt this was where Daniel had come.

He looked back at the car a good three hundred feet down the road and saw Carin standing by the front fender writing in her three-ring binder. Would she think he was as crazy as Rick? Would she see what he saw here? Or would she start spouting some gibberish about a psychic happening?

He didn't care right now. He took off at a jog to the car and as he approached it, Carin closed her notebook and looked up at him. "Are you ready to head for the airport?" she asked, her eyes hidden behind the sunglasses again.

He shook his head. "No."

She stood straight. "Where do you want me to drop you?"

"Nowhere, not just yet. You won't believe this, but I think I found Hell's Way."

Her mouth dropped open. "What?"

"It's here, right here. If we hadn't stopped, we would have gone right past it."

She looked around and shook her head. "What are you talking about?"

He almost took her by the arm to urge her out onto the highway so she could get a clear look at the formation, but thought better of it. Instead, he went around to get in behind the wheel of the car. "Come on. I'll show you."

He started the engine, and as she got in, he slipped the car into gear. He drove slowly onto the highway, then approached the formation. As he turned onto the shoulder to nose in toward the dirt trail, he stopped and pointed just ahead of them. "There it is."

She looked up, then slowly slipped off her sunglasses and her eyes skimmed over the formation. "Are you sure this is it?"

"I think it is."

She looked at him, the deep navy of her eyes unsettling him. "But do you *know* it is?"

He answered truthfully. "I know it is."

She didn't argue, or ask for explanations. Instead, she simply said, "Rick said that the first one knew, and you'd know too."

He didn't argue with her. There wasn't anything left in him to sustain anger at her. Not after the kiss. And not now that he'd literally found his needle in a haystack. "However it happened, we're here."

"What now?"

"It's going to be dark in half an hour, but I wish we could drive up the road a short way just to see what's up there."

"Why can't we?"

"In a brand new BMW? This isn't exactly a four-by-four Jeep."

"It's a car, and it's insured. Let's go and see what's up at Hell's Way."

"Are you sure?"

"Go for it."

He put the car in gear, then slowly started under the rock formation onto the trail that was sided by craggy walls that all but blocked what was left of the light. David flicked on the headlights and kept going on the road that cut through the butte, twisting and turning as if whatever had cut it had taken the path of least resistance. After about two hundred yards, with dust billowing out behind the BMW, they drove into a canyon that was rimmed on all sides by the walls of the butte.

It was no more than a mile across, and without a sign of life anywhere. There were a few clusters of low-growing trees dotting the land. David stopped the car in the middle of the area and as he looked around, he said, "It's a box canyon."

"Without any other opening?"

"It looks like it. And if this is Hell's Way, what is it?"

"Rick said that Daniel wanted to camp. And this would be a private place to do that, wouldn't it?"

"I suppose so." He looked at the stony walls that rimmed it and a full moon just rising in the night sky. "I guess it could make a camping site."

"Do you think this is where Daniel went after he left Crazy Rick's?"

He knew it was, but he wasn't about to say that to Carin. It just didn't make sense that nothing was here. "It could be," he hedged.

"It fits, that's for sure," Carin said. "But how did we find it? You didn't know it was here, and I sure didn't."

"Coincidence," he murmured, not about to examine that right now.

Carin gripped the front window frame with both hands and stood in the car to scan the area. Then she pointed to the west. "Look over there, by those trees."

David followed her motion and saw shadows that he couldn't quite make out. "What is it?"

"I don't know. Let's drive over there."

David turned the car as Carin sat back down, and he drove slowly across the rough ground. His headlights flashed ahead and he could see something near a clump of trees. As he got closer to the hillside, he knew they'd found a campsite. A huge area had been cut out of the wall of the canyon, going back maybe twenty feet under an overhang, a protection from the sun and the elements. The headlights showed a fire ring near the middle of it, a circle of large stones with what looked like the remnants of charred wood in the middle. A spreading tree off to one side probably shaded the area during the day.

David stopped the car with the lights right on the campsite and let the motor idle. There wasn't a sign of anyone around anywhere. "Now what?" he asked.

Carin got out and looked back at David. "Let's look around, then decide what to do."

As she walked in the glare of the lights toward the camp area, David turned off the engine, but left on the lights. Then he got out and headed after her. By the time he caught up to her, she was nudging at the campfire remnants with the toe of her sandal. "It's cold. No one's been here for awhile."

David went past the fire ring and looked at the crude wall of the hollowed-out area. The rock had been literally ground away, a process that must have taken aeons to do by hand, and wood had been packed into any exposed dirt areas. He went closer to the outside wall and stared at figures on the stones. "I think people like Rick have been here a lot," he said, and sensed Carin come to stand by his right shoulder and look past him at the wall.

"A peace sign," she said, then moved forward, her elbow bumping his arm as she got closer to a drawing on the wall. A skeleton with a rose in its hand and wearing a top hat. "Grateful Dead?"

"Looks like it," David said, then moved farther down the wall, past initials and dates, some going back almost eight years. Then he stopped. "Rick left his mark," he said. The name Ricky had been scratched into the stone and just below it was a perfect outline of a marijuana leaf.

Carin came over to him and looked at the wall. "You found it," Carin said and turned to look at him.

The bright lights from the car shone on her face and he could see the way she was looking at him. "Don't look at me like that. I swear, this whole thing is crazy," he said quickly.

"But you found this place. How did you do it?"

He didn't have any idea. "It's luck, pure and simple.

"Do you believe that?"

"What do you think it is?"

"You know what I think it is," she said directly.

He did know, and he wasn't about to discuss it with her. "And you know what I think about that."

"Of course I do."

"Then we know where we both stand."

"Absolutely." She moved away from him. "What do we do now?" she asked, looking at the wall again.

"I wish we could see things around here more clearly." She turned to him. "Then let's wait until daylight and look some more."

"In case you didn't notice, there aren't any motels in the vicinity."

"The car's here. The seats recline fully, and..." she walked out from under the overhang "...the sky's full of stars."

He hated to think of trying to spend a night with Carin sleeping close to him. But he hated to admit that she made sense. That was something she seemed to do regularly and it annoyed him. "Just camp out?"

"I've got blankets in the trunk and some bottled water. I come prepared for anything. Why not? It would save the time it would take to go and find someplace then come back in the morning."

More common sense. "You don't happen to have any food hidden away, do you?"

"Trail mix in the glove compartment."

"What kind?"

"The kind with raisins and nuts in it."

"Sold."

"Good." She started back to the car, and when she turned off the headlights, the full moon cast a pale glow all around. The scent of wild buckwheat drifted on the warm air. Slowly he headed back to the car, and he found Carin standing by the passenger door holding the blankets. "Which side do you want?"

He went around to the driver's side and got in behind the wheel. "This is fine," he said and found the seat adjustment. As the back lowered, he stretched out and stared at the sky over him. "What a night."

Carin got in the other seat and put the blankets on the small backseat. "The blankets are there if you need them later on. It might get chilly before dawn."

"Thanks."

He heard her open the glove compartment, then sit back and lower her seat. He turned to his right and saw her not more than a foot from him. "Here," she said, and held out a package of granola. "It was fresh two days ago, and it stays good for a long time."

He took the package, ripped it open and began to eat the mix. The grains tasted overly sweet, but he ate half of the package before twisting it closed and setting it on the console between them. Shifting to get more comfortable, he closed his eyes. "This desert seems to go on forever, doesn't it?"

"It's the biggest desert in the country," she murmured.

"More trivia?"

"Of course."

"Why is a doctor so fluent in trivia?"

"My mother used to say I was a human sponge. I didn't remember the big things, but tell me something that didn't make an iota of difference in anything, and I'd remember it years later. How about you? Do you have any peculiar habits or traits?"

He shifted in the seat, uncomfortable with the immediate answer that came to him. Just getting involved with strange doctors. That brought a smile to his lips. She wasn't strange. She was unique, but not strange.

"How about it? Are you asleep?"

He shifted until his shoulder was turned to her, and he said, "I was just thinking that I owe you an apology."

At least she didn't ask what the apology was for. Instead, she said softly, "No you don't."

"I do and I'm sorry." Even as he said the words, he knew the magnitude of that lie. Sorry wasn't what he felt. Maybe fear, maybe uncertainty, but nothing that approached regret for kissing her.

"It shouldn't have happened, but it did. And we'll just have to forget about it," she said, her voice soft on the night air.

"You're right," he agreed, but wondered if there was enough time in his life to forget.

He knew she'd made his whole life different. And as he touched his tongue to his lips, certain he'd find her taste still there, he felt his body begin to tighten. If he stayed here like this right now, he wouldn't get any sleep at all.

He sat up and reached behind him for one of the blankets. "There isn't much room in here. I'll just stretch out by the fire ring."

"That won't be very comfortable."

"It'll be fine," he said, knowing it would be even more uncomfortable for him if he tried to sleep this close to her.

"Here, take this," she said.

He looked down at her, the moonlight silvering her features, making her look almost ethereal. She was holding the other blanket out to him. "You'll need that," he said.

"I've got more if I need a cover."

He took the blanket and got out of the car. Closing the door behind him, he turned from her, crossing through the night to the fire ring. He shook out one blanket, stretched out on it and balled the other blanket under his head for a pillow. As he looked overhead, at stars that sprayed across the clear sky, he wondered if Daniel had lain like this, studying the stars overhead, feeling the balmy desert breeze skim across his skin.

He wondered again how he'd found Hell's Way, such as it was. Instinct, probably. An overactive imagination. That brought a slight smile. No one had ever accused him of having an overactive imagination. That was Daniel's territory.

He closed his eyes, crossed his arms on his chest, and let himself relax. It was definitely easier to relax twenty feet away from Carin.

He drifted off into sleep, feeling relief to be able to stop thinking and just rest.

HE HAD NO IDEA how long he'd been asleep when the nightmare came again.

Cold was everywhere, then heat. Burning. David could feel the scorch of fire near him, yet it didn't touch the cold that made his body ache.

Pain mingled with the fire, ripping through him, pressing on his chest and exploding with each beat of his heart. Then the cold came through a darkness unbroken by any light. A sound echoed through him, a thumping, up and down, over and over again. And every time the sound came, pain exploded inside his lungs.

"Let's hope it's not too bad," someone said, the woman who seemed to be talking through a long tunnel.

"It doesn't look good," a man said. "We've got to stop it now."

Through the fire, ice touched him on his head, at his hands and feet, along his sides and he began to shake uncontrollably. Each breath jarred his body and pressed against a steel band that encircled his chest.

"This should work," the man said. "But, stay with him."

"I will," the woman whispered. "I won't let him go."

But even as she echoed the words, David felt an icy cold surround him, threatening to bury him.

"Don't, don't," he breathed, "Don't, please, don't let me go."

And miraculously he felt warm hands on him, then arms around him. Anchored. That was the single word that came through the horror of the dream.

"David," the voice whispered, "David, it's all right."

He reached out to the woman, felt her under his hands, and he pulled her to him.

"David?" The voice, soft and close, so close, someone to hold on to, someone to anchor him and not let him drift away. He held on to her for dear life.

Chapter Eight

Carin woke with a start and for a moment she couldn't think of where she was. As she opened her eyes to a sky touched with traces of dawn and heat just beginning to touch her face, she heard David yell, "Don't! Don't leave me!"

She scrambled to sit up and free herself of the blanket tangling around her legs. She tossed it onto the backseat, then hurried out of the car and took off at a dead run for David.

He was on the ground, entangled in his blankets, his arms flailing. His voice echoed off the walls of the canyon, making it seem as if it echoed from the sky. "Don't, no!" As she got to David, she dropped to her knees and reached out, grabbing him by one arm. "It's all right. David? David. It's all right. You're dreaming."

Right then he froze and his eyes opened, but she knew they were still seeing the horror of his nightmare. "David," she whispered, leaning over him. "David?"

Slowly, his hand raised. Unsteadily, he touched her cheek, then with a groan that echoed in the air, he drew her down to him. And she didn't fight it. She let him pull her to his chest, let him bury his fingers in her tangled hair. She let him hold on to her.

While his heart thundered wildly against her cheek, and his chest rose and fell rapidly with each ragged breath, she closed her eyes. His hold on her was almost suffocating, but she didn't move or try to get free. Whatever the nightmare was, she knew the terror was still with him. Her need to help was as suffocating as his hold on her.

She hated suffering or pain in any one. But as David held her, she knew it was more than that with this man. It had been more since the first time he'd touched her. And now she wanted to take his pain, to shield him and help him. Her thought finished just as he framed her face with his hands and gently moved her until she was looking down at him.

She wanted to make love with him. She wanted to be with him here and now in this place. She met the look from his hooded eyes and breathing became impossible. He needed to hold her, she knew that, but she needed to get closer to him just as badly. She touched his jaw with the tips of her fingers, hating the unsteadiness there, and she breathed, "I'm here."

"I know," he whispered and drew her back to him, for his lips to capture hers.

And she went to him, opening her mouth, inviting him in, needing a contact with this man that had no definition. His taste and essence filled her, and she moved closer to him, amazed at how easily her body molded to his and how right it felt.

This was new to her, something she'd never felt before, and as the caress deepened, Carin felt herself melt. If she could have, she would have let herself go into David, to be absorbed into his being and become one with him.

His hands set fire to her body, sending a desire through her that shocked and excited her. This had never happened with any of the men who had flitted through her life. And with David there was no hedging her bets.

When his hand found her breast through the thin cotton of her top, a throbbing started deep in her being, a knot that coiled tighter and tighter as his fingers massaged her nipple to a hard bud. Then the material was being tugged up, and David rolled her onto her back, putting himself over her. His mouth took the place of his hand.

As he drew her nipple into his mouth, into heat and warmth, she threw her head back, arching toward the caress. "Beautiful, absolutely beautiful," she heard him breathe as his mouth found her other breast. Beautiful. Yes, it was beautiful, and terrifying in its intensity.

No man had touched her like this and made her think about infinite possibilities, and no man had ever made her feel as if the world had ground to a stop. Comforting him was the last thing she was thinking about. Need. Desire. But not comfort. She grabbed at his shirt, needing to feel his skin under hers, and as she tugged the cotton free of his pants, she opened her eyes.

David was over her, looking down at her, and as his hand moved to the fastener at the waist of her shorts, her hands stilled. The expression in his eyes was touched with a desperation that stopped her dead.

He wasn't seeing her. Not the real her. He wasn't seeing a woman who disagreed with him, who wanted to study him, a woman who had originally come with him to see his interaction with his twin. He was seeing a lifeline, maybe a dream, but not her. He'd said he hated lies, and she knew that she did, too. There was no way she could take what he was offering when it would all be a lie.

She covered his hand at her waistband with hers, and bit her lip hard. "No," she managed, then moved jerkily to one side, away from David and his touch.

Oh God, she felt as if she had denied every good thing in life, and it made her feel vaguely sick to her stomach. She grabbed at her top, tugging it over her throbbing breasts, and stared at the dusty ground beyond the fire ring. She had no idea what to say. The woman who never stopped talking didn't have a single word that could make things right or make logic out of havoc.

"Carin?" she heard David say.

She bit her lip, then took a shaky breath and made herself say the only words she could think of to make a grasp at sanity. "You apologized last night. It's my turn." She sat up, careful not to look at David. "You were calling out and I didn't think." She tried to laugh, but it came out as little more than a nervous exhale. "I thought I could help, but..." She scrambled to her feet and without looking back, hurried toward the car.

She busied herself putting the seats back up and straightening the inside. When she found her sunglasses, she put them on, and only then did she look back to where David was. The blankets had been folded and David was crouched by the wall, studying it.

As he straightened, Carin looked away and barely kept herself from going back to him.

DAVID LINGERED at the wall, blindly staring at initials and drawings. But his mind never quite focused past what had happened between himself and Carin. His body sure wouldn't let him forget it. He tried to focus on the wall, skimming over the faded imprints. Nothing. Not a sign of Daniel. Maybe he was being drawn into Carin's thinking, into the crazy mind-link theory. He shook his head. He sure as hell was being drawn into other crazy things with this lady.

He straightened up. For as long as he could remember, he'd been on his own. Twin or not, he didn't buy into that half-of-a-whole theory. Daniel had his life, David had his. He loved his brother, but Daniel wasn't his anchor in this world, not any more than he could make Carin an anchor in this madness.

The moment she'd drawn back from him, he'd realized he'd been holding on to her to keep him from fragmenting. A lingering craziness from the dream. As he braced himself to turn and go back to the car, knowing he'd hit a dead end, he spotted something bright that glinted in the sun near the base of the wall.

He moved to it, hunkered down and picked up a quarter. He looked at it and saw particles of stone powder on its edge, then he looked directly above where he found it and saw something cut into the rock near the base. T. J. P. He almost dropped the quarter as he got to his feet and turned to call out to Carin.

"He's been here," he called as he saw her by the car, the sun catching golden streaks in her hair as she bent over the notebook in her hand.

She looked up at the sound of his voice, then tossed the notebook into the car and headed back to him. The sight of her jogging toward him, her hair lifting away from her face, her legs moving easily, her breasts moving gently with each step, brought back the tightness. He turned from her as she got closer. Enough, he told himself. Enough.

"What is it?" she asked in a breathless voice.

He motioned to the initials scratched into the stone. "I would have missed it, except I saw this quarter and when I went to pick it up..." He let his words trail off as Carin crouched at the wall, her slender finger touching the initials in the stone.

"T. J. P.?"

"T. J. Pierce. I told you he often takes on that persona when he's figuring out a story. Maybe he's using this place in the book and made the mark."

"So, this really is Hell's Way, and Daniel was here." She stood and turned to him, not more than a foot of space separating them. "It's like a miracle that you found it at all, and to find this on the wall... It's unbelievable, isn't it?"

He blinked, trying to minimize the effect her closeness was having on him and the way her words bothered him. "Let's call it another coincidence."

"If you like," she murmured, a frown tugging at her finely arched eyebrows.

"Maybe it's something more—I don't know," he admitted as his hand tightened on the quarter.

"I believe in miracles," she said looking into his eyes.

He knew he was starting to believe just a bit, and that was almost as unsettling as what had happened with Carin. "All right, Daniel was here." He exhaled. "Now we need a miracle to figure out where he went from here."

"We got this far," she said simply.

"Exactly. And now where do we go from here?"

She combed her hair back from her face with both hands, then stared up at the sky, the sweep of her throat exposed and vulnerable. And David could still taste her on his tongue, the hot essence of her skin, and his body responded without missing a beat.

He turned from her, staring blindly around the box canyon. "Let's get out of here and decide what to do while we drive to Tucson." He closed his eyes for a long moment, then opened them to find that Carin had moved around him and was already on her way to the car.

"Don't forget the blankets," she called over her shoulder.

He deliberately turned from the sight of her, knowing that the image of her right now was so burned into his brain that he didn't have to look at her to remember. He scooped up the blankets and headed for the car.

"When we get to a phone, I'd like to try Daniel's place," he said as he reached the car.

"You know, I've got a phone in the car, but it won't get any signal with these ridges all around," Carin said as she folded the blanket she'd used during the night.

"They work off these microwave dishes and if the signal can't go straight, it doesn't get to the phone."

He should have known she'd have a cellular phone in a car like this. "Where is it?"

"In the console."

"Why didn't you tell me you had it before?"

"You never asked, and I never thought about it until now," she said simply. "We always found pay phones where we stopped."

He wasn't any match for her brand of logic. "When we get away from here I'll try to call Daniel's home. Maybe he'll be there."

"Maybe," she said as she went around to open the trunk. As she tossed the blanket inside, David crossed to her and put his blankets on top of hers.

"How would you feel if he answered the phone?" he asked.

Her hands stilled on the dusty trunk lid and she looked at David, those glasses in place again. "I'd be relieved. How do you think I'd feel?"

"I don't know, but it would throw a monkey wrench in your theories if Daniel was sitting on the houseboat right now writing his book, wouldn't it?"

Her expression tightened, and she slammed the trunk lid down. "Believe it or not, I'd be thrilled if he was."

Had he thought he could distance himself from her by getting back to why she was on this trip? If so, he'd failed miserably. All it had accomplished was to put high color in her cheeks and remind him that her blushing drove him crazy.

Without a word he went around the car to get in behind the wheel. "All right if I drive again?" he asked.

"I don't care," Carin said and went around to the passenger side of the car.

He felt like a heel, and any excitement at finding T. J. P. cut into the stone was dissolving rapidly. He'd never felt more confused.

He touched the key, but didn't start the car. "What do you really think happened to my brother?"

When she didn't answer, he turned to her, seeing her putting her notebook back in her briefcase. As she did up the zipper, she looked at David. "I don't have a clue. No mind flashes, no intuitive insights, and no psychic answers."

"I know, I know," he muttered as she threw his own words back at him. "I was being honest back there," he said, turning from her. He held on to the top of the steering wheel and stared at the gouge in the rock wall.

"No you weren't."

He exhaled. Of course he wasn't being honest with Carin. Dammit, if he was totally honest, he'd have to tell her that coming with her had been a monumental mistake. Touching her, kissing her, had been an even bigger mistake, and if he was honest, he'd tell her that he wanted to take her here and now, and never look back.

"What are you talking about?" he asked, his voice low and edged with hoarseness.

"Are you going to tell me what that was all about back there?"

A bull's-eye hit. It almost took the air right out of him. "I'm not in the habit of apologizing for finding a woman attractive."

"I wasn't talking about that."

"Then what?"

"What was the dream all about?"

He gripped the steering wheel. "A nightmare. That's all." He shrugged.

"You said you never dreamed."

"I never used to." He started the car, hoping that if they were driving away from this place, that he could think more clearly. "But, these are strange times, aren't they?"

"Won't you tell me what it was all about?"

"I don't remember," he said, surprised at how easily the lies came now. "Poof, gone. Nothing to analyze. And I don't want to go over and over this."

"I used to have nightmares when I was little. There was one about an aunt of mine who died when I was little, and she kept trying to visit me, you know, her ghost. I told my mother and she said that sometimes ghosts tried to contact people."

"Your mother told you that?" he asked, his hand on the gearshift.

"Yes, and she told me how to deal with it."

He looked at her finally, thankful she was looking down at the seat belt buckle as she tried to fasten it.

"How?"

She snapped her seat belt and tugged at the strap over her shoulder. "She said to sit on the bed Indian-style, turn out the lights and say very clearly, 'I'm not afraid of ghosts, I'm not afraid of ghosts' ten times."

"And the ghost was miraculously gone?"

She looked at him. "Oh, I didn't want her gone, I just wanted to understand what was happening."

He rolled his eyes upward. "Good God, no wonder you buy into that psychic stuff."

"I dealt with it," she said, "and my mother helped. I admit that she's a bit odd at times, but it worked."

"What worked, séances, voodoo or chanting?"

She crossed her arms on her chest. "My mother just taught me a valuable lesson."

"What?"

"There's more to life than meets the eye or can be experienced with the five senses."

As she adjusted her glasses, he realized that he hated not seeing her eyes, but conceded that it was probably better right now that he wasn't making direct contact. "And you, as a doctor, buy into that?"

"I believe it. And it's not because of my mother."

"What about your father?"

"What about him?"

"Does he believe it?"

She nodded. "Yes, he does."

"Is your whole family crazy?"

She smiled not offended at all, but making it harder and harder on him to keep his hands on the steering wheel. "I told you, my sister's a pediatrician and knows there's more to this life than the physical. My father's a retired army general, a man made to go by the rules. He's open to it. And my mother's an artist. You know about her."

"Quite a family."

"Yours isn't exactly normal, now is it?"

"Daniel's a bit eccentric at times."

"And your mother's been married umpteen times to screwballs."

He smiled. She'd pegged his mother exactly. "Touché."

"I don't think that there are any so-called normal people in this world. Just being human automatically exempts most people from coming close to normal. I'm not even close. I told you that before." She cocked her head to one side. "Know what?"

"What?"

"You're not normal, either, even though I've got a gut feeling that you think you're probably the last normal man on earth."

His smile faltered. "Thanks for the assessment, but I thought we made a deal not to psychoanalyze each other."

"You're right. I'm sorry." She reached for her cotton cap, twisted her hair up and tugged the hat over it. As she pulled the front down a bit, she looked at David. "So, let's get going. I'd kill for a hot shower and fresh clothes right about now."

He'd kill for some peace of mind. As he moved to put the car in gear, he glanced in the rearview mirror and froze. A dust cloud that rose more than thirty feet in the air was obscuring the opening back to the road. In the next instant he heard the throbbing drone of unmuffled engines.

"What's that?" Carin asked, twisting in the seat to look behind them. But David kept his eyes on the rearview mirror.

"We've got visitors," he muttered.

As he watched, a full-dress Harley ridden by the biggest, meanest-looking biker he'd ever seen rode out of the dust. The man was huge. He was wearing what looked like a skullcap of leather, partially covering long gray hair that matched a full beard. Wraparound sunglasses glinted back the morning sun, and a black leather vest exposed darkly tanned arms that had the circumference of a tree trunk. Behind him came two more bikes, both with double riders, all without helmets and all dressed in matching leather vests fastened with chains, torn jeans and heavy boots.

David heard Carin take in a shocked breath as she got a good look at them. "They look like something out of the movie *Easy Rider.*"

"Too bad none of them even vaguely resembles Dennis Hopper or Peter Fonda," he murmured, never taking his eyes off the obvious leader.

He'd thought the man was big at first sight, but as the man rode closer to the BMW, David conceded that the man looked like a human mountain. Hundreds of pounds of machine and man. David stared into the rearview mirror and watched the bikes come close to the car, then fan out to surround it.

Any hope that they'd keep going or turn and go back the way they'd come was shot down as they started riding in circles around the car. The heavy throbbing of the engines mingled in the hot air with dust and the smell of fumes.

When Carin touched his arm, David jumped. "What are they doing?" she asked, her voice almost swallowed up in the heavy throbbing of the engines.

"I don't know, but you did say this car's fully insured, didn't you?"

"Yes, of course, but—"

"Is your seat belt fastened?"

"David?"

"Is it?" he cut in as the dusty circle of bikes began to close in on the car.

"Yes, yes it is." Her fingers were biting in to his forearm now. "What are you going to do?"

"Just what you suggested at Crazy Rick's." He looked at her, unnerved by the fear he saw in her expression, and he experienced a surge of an emotion that he could only call protectiveness. A new emotion for him. "We're going to make a run for it," he said with more conviction than he felt."

"Don't you think that maybe they're just sort of toying with us?"

"We're cut off completely, and I doubt that there's anyone else within ten miles. This isn't some movie, and they aren't playing parts."

When she looked at him, the sun caught on her sunglasses. "Believe it or not, I'm a realist when I have to be. Just tell me what we're going to do."

"I wish this was a bigger car and not a convertible, but it's going to have to do. I'll try to gun the car backward, spin in a hundred-and-eighty-degree arch and drive like hell for the road."

The bikes suddenly came to a stop. As the dust settled, David saw the leader had stopped ahead of them and was facing the car. He knew he had to do something and do it now, but when he would have shifted the car into reverse, Carin let go of his arm only to cover his hand on the gearshift with hers. "You can't go backward," she whispered. "One of them's right behind us."

He glanced in the mirror. One of the bikers, a tall, thin man who was completely bald and had a large blue teardrop tattooed on his forehead had parked not more then ten feet behind the BMW. "It's your call," David said to Carin as he watched the man behind them. "Either I back up and to hell with the bald one, or I take on that mountain."

She took a sharp breath. "The big one's getting off his bike." Her hand fumbled with his until their fingers were intertwined. She held on to him for dear life.

David looked ahead as the man got off, hit the kickstand, steadied his machine, then turned to the car. He was just as big off the bike as he'd looked on it. He stood ramrod straight, his full height probably six foot six or seven, and he wasn't fat. Just huge.

His salt-and-pepper hair hung around beefy shoulders, and his leather vest held together with chains couldn't hide a massive chest that looked as if it was covered with tattoos. Frayed jeans were tucked into well-worn calf-high motorcycle boots with chains wrapped around the ankles.

"Crazy Rick on steroids," he muttered while the man stared at them for what seemed an eternity.

"Maybe we can talk to him," Carin said, and she was so close that he could have sworn he felt the heat of her breath on his neck.

"If there's *any* chance to talk, let me do it."

"And if that doesn't work?"

"Then I'll do whatever I have to do," he said, knowing it was probably the most honest thing he'd said to Carin. If he had to, he'd gun the car directly back, to hell with the consequences. He'd never taken on a Sir Galahad mantle in his life. That had been Daniel's forte, not his. But since Carin had walked into the houseboat, he'd been doing things that were way outside his comfort zone. He almost laughed. Comfort zone? There hadn't been a suggestion of a comfort zone since he'd found out there was a Dr. Carin Walker in this world.

"Do you think he's got a gun?" she whispered, and he could feel her shoulder pressing against his arm. The console might never have existed, she was so close to him.

"I can't see one, but I don't think he needs one." The man had the biggest hands he'd ever seen. "Look at those hands. He doesn't need any other weapon."

The biker started toward the car, and as Carin's hold on David became numbing, she whispered, "Oh, God, we're going to die, aren't we?"

Chapter Nine

Before David could tell her she wouldn't die if he had anything to say about it, the leader got closer. He moved quickly for a man of his size, and before David could begin to untangle his hand from Carin's, he found himself looking straight up into the face of the human mountain.

Sunglasses hid the giant's eyes, but David could clearly see that the main tattoo on his chest where the vest was open read, The Kiss of Death. The man crossed his arms on his chest, arms that looked massive and sinewy with muscle. Backing up over the skinny one was definitely the better alternative for David.

But before he could get his hand free of Carin's so he could put the car in reverse, a remarkable thing happened. The beard twitched, and the man actually smiled. The next thing David knew, the man slipped off the sunglasses, exposing shadowed eyes under shaggy brows, then leaned forward and slapped the frame of the door with one huge hand. The car shook.

"Geez, man, you had me fooled." The voice matched the man's appearance. It was rock-deep and almost echoed with bass. Before David could do or say anything, the man held one hand in the air and gave the thumbs-up sign to the other bikers. Suddenly the bikes were turned off and the only sounds left were the BMW's motor and David's heart hammering in his chest. He held onto Carin.

The man moved back half a pace and eyed the BMW, then looked right at David. He'd seen that look before, a lot of times. The same look that had been in Willy's eyes at the restaurant. And when the man muttered, "A Beamer, a damn Beamer. Man, oh man, oh man. How the mighty have fallen," he knew he was right. He thought he was Daniel.

He sank back in the seat and prayed that Daniel hadn't made an enemy with this man.

"What happened to the machine?" the man asked as he put his glasses back on and leaned toward the car. His large hands gripped the door frame.

"The Harley?" David asked, weighing his options. Tell him he wasn't Daniel and chance the man turning on him? Or what if he went along with the guy, and the man figured it out, the way Crazy Rick had?

"What other, man? Of course your Harley." He shook his head. "A machine among machines." He looked past David at Carin, then reached one hand to slip his glasses down on his nose and look at her over the frames. "And a woman among women," he said softly.

David didn't miss the look of appreciation in the man's eyes.

"My name's Trig, and what's yours, sweetheart?"

Trig. He felt Carin squeeze his hand as she began to put the pieces of a puzzle together at the same time he did. First Hell's Way, now Trig. "You can call me Carin," Carin answered.

"Carin," the giant said, then looked at David over his glasses, before he stood back and pushed his glasses up into place. "When you were here the last time, you said there wasn't any ball and chain in the picture."

Carin leaned around David and looked up at the man. "Ball and chain?" she asked.

"You prefer 'old lady'?" he asked with total seriousness.

"I prefer Carin," she said.

"Carin it is." He turned and motioned the others over to the car. "Come on over. It's T. J., and he's got a Carin with him."

T. J.? Daniel had used his character's name with this man? David darted Carin a look, but she was staring past him at Trig. When David followed her gaze, he saw Trig had turned to say something to one of the other bikers, and David could see the back of the man's leather vest. A logo on it was faded, but he could make out a large red circle filled with a skull and crossbones with blood coming out of its eyes. Splashed in a sweep across it in lightning bolt lettering was Hell's Way Forever.

This must have been the meeting ground for the gang, and Daniel had found it with the help of Crazy Rick. Trig turned back to David. "How did you know we'd be here?"

"I didn't." He took a breath and knew there wasn't any point in pretending to be Daniel. There was no way he could keep up that charade and get any information out of the man. "I'm not Dan . . . T. J."

He frowned and leaned in toward David, both hands gripping the frame of the car door again. "What's that?"

"I'm T. J.'s brother."

He waited, watching, hoping he wouldn't be torn limb from limb. He was getting to really hate sunglasses. The eyes being the windows to the soul really rang true for him, and he hated not being able to see past the tinted lenses and read the man's reaction to his announcement.

"You're who?" Trig finally asked.

David was aware of the other bikers coming closer, on either side of Trig. But he never looked away from his own reflection in the man's glasses. "I'm T. J.'s brother, his twin brother."

The man was so still, David wondered if he was contemplating pillaging and plundering. Then he stood back, crossing his arms on his chest, revealing a tattoo of blue snake wound around his massive forearm, with the words, Die Trying scrolled in a banner on his wrist. David didn't think the man was the type to discuss things rationally.

"If you aren't T. J., did he send you here?"

"No, Crazy Rick did."

"No way. Rick can tell you every part ever made for a vintage Harley, but he'd be hard put to figure out up from down. And you're telling me he told you how to find this place?"

Carin let go of David to lean around him so she could look up at Trig. She braced herself with her hand on David's thigh, and he found himself closing his eyes at the contact. "Rick said that Hell's Way could heal auras. He said to go under it, to find healing. He said—"

"What in the hell does that all mean?"

She hesitated. "We didn't really understand it, but we found Hell's Way, and we—"

"I'd say you two were found, not the ones finding," Trig cut in.

Carin moved back, taking her hand off his thigh. David opened his eyes. She had moved back farther, as if she had realized she needed distance between herself and Trig. "What do you mean?"

Trig motioned to his right, to the bald man who had blocked the car at the rear. "Meet Scat." Then he nodded toward the other man. "And Pec. Dody is Pec's old lady, and Gem is Scat's old lady. Being as how we're Hell's Way, I'd say we sort of found you two, wouldn't you?"

Carin stared at the man. "You're a . . . a gang?"

"We prefer to be called a family."

"You're Hell's Way?"

"Us and about twenty more, and have been for over fifteen years."

She'd so wanted David to have that link with Daniel that she'd been more than ready to believe that this place was Hell's Way. But one way or the other, David got them here. "Rick said you could heal auras. I don't suppose you do?" Carin asked.

Trig smiled. "No, we're not into peyote, or other mind-benders. Poor old Rick took one trip too many. Our drug of choice is freedom, and maybe a touch of pot now and then."

She sank back in the seat and rested her arm on the window frame. This was something more than she'd thought would happen. David hadn't found this place by coincidence or even luck. There was more to it than that. It had been one chance in a million to find it out here in the middle of nowhere. And Daniel had been here with these people.

If they hadn't stopped, if David hadn't walked from the car, if they hadn't kissed, if...? She looked at David and knew she'd found an inkling of what she'd been looking for. Someway, somehow, he was being drawn to Daniel, or at least, after Daniel.

"What'd you say you're called?" Trig was saying to David.

"I'm David."

"Well, David, since Rick promised we could heal auras, why don't we give it a shot?" He pulled the car door open. "Let's commune."

"What?"

"Let's sit and talk. Do you smoke?"

"Smoke?"

"Cigarettes."

"No, I gave them up two years ago."

"I should, but I haven't, so come and sit while I have one." He leaned down to get closer. "You can tell me what the hell you're doing here, and why you hunted down Crazy Rick and why you thought this canyon was Hell's Way, okay?"

"Sure," David said and got out.

Carin got out too, and by the time she'd closed the door and turned, Trig was right beside her. He casually slipped his arm around her shoulder, and she felt as if she was being swallowed up. "Come on, beautiful. Get you out of this sun," he said, leading her over toward the shelter by the fire ring.

After the foul mixture that clung to Rick, it was a pleasant surprise that Trig smelled of leather, fresh air, and a touch of gasoline and motors. "You...you come here often?" she asked as she walked with him.

He squeezed her shoulder. "Off and on. Damn glad we stopped by this morning, though. Didn't know there was a great-looking lady waiting for me."

Carin looked at David who was coming up beside her. And even without making eye contact, he seemed to sense her uneasiness. Casually, he reached for her hand, lacing his fingers with hers, and looked at Trig over her head. "She's with me."

When Trig stopped and looked over at David, Carin wondered if they'd jumped from the frying pan into the fire. The others stopped where they were, watching, waiting. Then slowly, Trig took his arm from around Carin. "No problem. You should have said she was yours."

"Yeah, well, she is," David said. His hold on Carin tightened, but his voice stayed even.

Trig smiled. "Can't blame a guy for trying, can you?"

"No, you sure can't," David said.

Trig motioned to the fire ring. "Let's sit down, and you tell me a story about your brother while I roll a smoke."

The others headed for the fire ring and Carin and David followed. "Thanks," she whispered just for him to hear.

He squeezed her shoulder, then let her go. "I think you'd better play the part while we're here."

"Part?" she asked as they neared the fire ring.

When she looked at him, he motioned with his eyes to the others as they settled by the ring. The two men sat in front, sitting Indian-style facing the ring, while the two women sat behind them.

"Two steps behind?" she murmured.

"At least," David said and headed for the empty spot by Trig.

Carin hesitated, then as Trig turned to look at her, she didn't have to see his eyes to know what David suggested was smart. What Trig thought was important was the only thing that mattered right now.

She crossed to where David was sitting, and she went behind him, then dropped to her knees and sat back on her heels. While David settled in front of her, she watched Trig. The man took his time rolling a cigarette, then as he lit it, he looked at David. "All right, man, tell me what's going on."

While David explained about Daniel's disappearance, Trig took long drags on the cigarette and let the smoke trickle out his mouth and nose. Even though they were in the shade of the overhang, Carin could feel the heat building and the morning breeze merely stirring it rather than relieving the heat.

She felt dampness in her hair under the cap, and a trickle of moisture ran down between her breasts. The others in the group looked impervious to the heat, despite the leather they were wearing. No one but Trig smoked, and no one but David and Trig spoke.

"Quite a story," Trig said as he ground out the cigarette in the sand, then flicked it into the fire ring. "What do you want from me?"

"Did Daniel say where he was going when he left here?"

"He just said he was wandering around. He was here two days, then took off early one morning. Said, 'see ya,' and headed out."

"What did he do for those two days?"

"Asked a lot of questions and listened to the history of Hell's Way, how we came about, how we got here, and what we do."

"That's it?"

"He was obsessed with the history of the canyon."

"This place?"

"Yeah. The Indians used to call it the Canyon of Living Shadows. Now it's just Shadow Canyon."

Another part of the puzzle. Shadows.

"What other questions did he ask?"

"All sorts." Trig exhaled. "The man was one question after the other. He never stopped." He shook his head. "The guy even wanted to know about the bars."

"What bars?"

"You know, bars, drinking and dancing. He wanted to know where he could go and find bars that catered to bikers. Any bar on the southern route into New Mexico."

"Did you give him the names of any?"

Carin didn't remember any bar names in the notes. "Hell, sure. If anyone'd know that, I would. I gave him six or seven places to check out."

David felt in his pockets, then turned to Carin. "I need some paper and a pen."

Carin didn't say a thing. She scrambled to her feet, hurried to the car, grabbed a pen and paper then hurried back to hand them to David. He took them and turned to Trig.

"What names and locations did you give him?"

"I'll tell you what I remember, and you write it down." Trig looked up at Carin, his sunglasses glinting back the sun high in the sky. "I bet you got an education," he said out of the blue.

She nodded. "Some."

"Me, I got kicked out of school in the ninth grade. I never did get back. I had to educate myself."

At places like this and bars, she thought, but said, "Self-education isn't all bad," she said.

"It gets me through." Trig looked at David. "Ready?"

"Go ahead."

While Trig reeled off names and places, Carin went to the wall and dropped down, pressing her back to the relative coolness of the rock. She studied each person in the group, from Trig the giant, to Pec, a fairly short man, but who looked like he was into heavy bodybuilding, and Scat with the teardrop tattoo.

The two women hadn't moved and hadn't said a word. They were two of a kind with long, dull hair caught back in low ponytails, and wearing leather, chains and denim. They could have been any age, from late teens to early thirties. Scat's "old lady" had a tattoo of a teardrop just like his, but on her shoulder exposed by the leather vest.

Trig got to his feet slowly, the giant unfolding until he was his full height, then David stood and came to Carin as he folded the piece of paper. He pushed both the paper and pen into the pocket of his shirt. "We're out of here," he said and reached out to take her hand as if it was the most natural thing in the world.

She started for the car with him, her fingers laced with his, then Trig fell in step beside her. "If you're smart, you'll find a man with a bike."

David's hand tightened on hers, but he didn't stop walking toward the car. "Excuse me?" Carin said to Trig.

"A bike. You know, face a fear and it's gone. That's the only way to get over being afraid of bikes."

When Carin would have stopped, David kept going, his hand tugging at hers to keep her by his side.

Trig leaned a bit closer to her as they headed for the car. "Having phobias isn't anything to be ashamed of."

"Of course not," she said, and wondered just what she'd missed in the conversation between David and Trig.

They got to the car and Trig reached to open the door for Carin. She slipped in, he closed it and braced himself on it to look down at her. "You know, if you got a fear, it's best to face it. If you want, we can work on it together."

"I don't think so," she said.

David got in behind the wheel, and reached over to catch Carin by the hand. "I'll help her with her fears."

Trig backed up while looking down at Carin. His glasses reflected her own face staring up at him. "If you ever want to get a bike between your legs, don't forget my offer," he said.

"Thanks, but I'll stick with David for now," she said.

Trig shrugged his massive shoulders, then moved toward his bike, got on, and kick started it. The other two men did the same. With the noise of their engines filling the air, Carin looked at David. "What was that all about? " He released her hand to start the car. "I thought he understood I wasn't available?"

"He heard me, but he hasn't given up wanting to ride off into the sunset with you on the back of his bike."

"So, you told him I was afraid of motorcycles?"

"I said that you had an ugly experience with a biker and hadn't been near a bike since."

"Couldn't you have just told him that I wasn't going to go with him? I hate the way they treat their women. My God, it is the twentieth century."

"No psychological explanation?" he asked.

"Of course. Women like that need a connection, any connection, to belong, but that doesn't make it right. I would have liked to have the chance to explain that to Trig and set him straight."

"Believe me, there are times when a good story is better than a confrontation with a human mountain no matter what he believes," he said and started the car. "I thought we agreed that he didn't need a gun to ruin a perfectly good day."

She sank back in the seat. He was right. She looked at Trig as he started toward the way out of the canyon. One of his men fell in behind Trig, and the other one, Scat, stayed where he was behind the BMW. When David swung the car around to head after them, Scat followed the car. "How long is the list of the bars?"

"Here." He took the piece of paper out of his pocket and handed it to Carin. "There's six names and rough directions. Daniel was looking for weird and I think Trig steered him in the right direction."

They eased onto the trail that led to the highway. "I didn't remember any names in the notebook that sounded like the names of bars."

"They weren't there. Daniel must have just figured if he saw one, he'd stop."

David slowly drove down the trail. "So, we'll try to find the bars as we go?"

"That's the plan."

She looked ahead at the bikes with Trig leading the way. "I really thought he was going to harm us when he first showed up."

"He still looks like he could," David murmured.

"It looks like Daniel was deliberately searching out people who are on the edge, one way or another."

"T. J. Pierce lives that kind of life, and Daniel's always done the same, living close to the edge."

"What about you?"

"What about me?" he asked as he turned on the air conditioner and adjusted the vent to blow right on his chest.

"How close to the edge do you get in your life?"

"How close do you think a professor of archaeology would get to the edge of life?"

"That's what I'm asking you."

"Two days ago I would have said the closest I came to risky behavior was going to an isolated dig during summer break with a group of overly enthusiastic students."

"And now?"

He shrugged. "One risk after another."

She slipped lower in the seat and tugged her hat down on her forehead. "Isn't that the truth."

"I guess the bottom line is any risk is a good risk if you survive."

"Sure, easy for you to be philosophical. You don't have some giant of a man wanting to make you his motorcycle moll."

"And I hope I never do." His chuckle was soft and as welcome as a cool breeze.

"Are you going to tell me what else went on back there?"

David cast her a quick look as he slowed to put a bit more distance between the car and the front bikes. "What?"

"What are you holding back?"

"Look who's asking? The one who wouldn't have ever told me what Rick said if I hadn't cornered you."

"That was different. Ever since I met you, I knew that you weren't the type to tell anyone everything. You always hold something back, always keep a part of yourself in reserve."

"Always analyzing, aren't you?"

"I guess I should have told you I'm obsessed with analyzing."

"I think I figured that out a while ago."

"So, what are you holding back now?"

He exhaled and looked ahead. "You're too smart for your own good."

"I should have told you that, too. Now, are you going to tell me the whole truth?"

"All right. You're a head doctor. You know your business and you're good at dealing with people."

She didn't know how to handle him, that was for sure. "Don't flatter me, David, just tell me what's going on."

"You haven't asked me where we're going," he said as they got to the highway, then turned right to follow Trig. Scat fell in behind them as they headed down the road.

"I thought we were heading for the bars."

"Not right away."

She sat straighter. "All right, where are we going right away?"

"To a motel near Tucson. Trig's showing us the way."

"Excuse me?"

"You said you wanted a hot shower and to change your clothes."

"Sure, but why do we have to go with them?"

"He offered."

"You didn't have to accept."

"Trig's like that old joke about where a gorilla sits. Anywhere he wants to. Well, this gorilla wanted to do this. He assured me he was going there anyway, so it wasn't any inconvenience."

"And?"

"We're going."

She sank back in the seat. "And you agreed to follow him to God knows where?"

"I know where we're going. It's a motel. He said he was meeting some people there before he headed south into Mexico."

"Then what are we going to do?"

"They're heading to Mexico, and we're heading for the bars."

She settled back in the seat and opened the piece of folded paper he'd handed to her. "Purgatory? Dev-

il's Playground? The Pit?'' She looked at David. ''Is
he serious about these places?''

"Daniel wanted to see them, so we'll go there too."

She refolded the paper, then handed it back to David. As he pushed it into his shirt pocket, she opened
the glove compartment and took out her sunscreen.
The noise of the throbbing engines vibrated in the air,
and the fumes seemed to be everywhere. Methodically Carin began to rub the lotion onto her arms and
legs.

Living on the edge? As she rubbed it on her thighs,
she knew she wasn't just approaching the edge, she
was close enough to fall over into a place she had never
been before.

WHEN AN HOUR WENT BY and they were skirting Tucson on an almost empty two-lane highway, David began to get uneasy. Trig kept going with Pec, and Scat
stayed right behind the BMW.

He glanced at Carin who had curled up on the seat,
her head resting against the back, one leg tucked under her and her hands clasped loosely on her lap. She
hadn't said a thing for so long, he thought she was
asleep. But she wasn't. She was waiting and watching. She sighed, shifted and tugged at the hem of her
shorts, but didn't look at him.

He knew that at any minute she'd look at him and
ask the same questions he was thinking about. And he
didn't have any answers. Hell, he didn't have answers
for a lot of questions that plagued him.

Why had she been engaged twice and backed out
twice? Why did she let him kiss her? Why did she
come to him this morning? Why couldn't he think

about much else except her and what she was doing to him?

He tried to shift his thoughts back to what Trig had told him just before they left Shadow Canyon. "We'll head for the motel to meet the others, and you two can rest up there before you head out," Trig had said. "And maybe I'll think of something else on the way there that T. J. told me that could help."

He wondered if the man had dangled that tidbit just to keep David hanging on.

When Tucson was well behind them, Carin finally stirred and David knew she was sitting straighter and looking at him.

"Where are we going?" she said, breaking into his confusion.

He didn't look at her. "I told you, to the motel," he said as they passed a scattering of houses interspersed with long stretches of empty, dry land.

"I thought you said Trig told you it was near Tucson."

He glanced in the rearview mirror, at Scat still right behind them, then past him to Tucson rapidly disappearing in the distance. "That's what he told me."

"What if there isn't a motel?"

He regripped the steering wheel. "If this motel doesn't miraculously appear in another ten miles, we'll tell Trig so long and head off on our own." He looked around at the landscape, the mesas off in the distance, and the scattering of houses and commercial buildings he could see. "To hell with the motel and the rest of the gang he's meeting there."

"The rest of the gang?" Carin echoed.

"He's meeting other gang members before going south."

"You mean we're following this man to a rendezvous with his gang, Hell's Way? Why didn't you tell me that?"

"I did, I—"

"You never mentioned anything about other gang members."

He couldn't remember if he'd used those words back at the canyon or not. He'd had more important things to worry about than filling in details for Carin. "It slipped my mind."

"Did anything else *slip* your mind?"

He glanced at her. She had turned in her seat with her back against the door, facing him. The bright sun hid nothing, not the line of her cheek, or the way her throat was exposed, or the rise and fall of her breasts under the tank top. "Nothing," he muttered, wishing the memory of holding her and touching her would slip his mind. But it wouldn't.

"What if Trig is leading us off into God knows where so the gang can—"

"We're on a main road. I'm not about to follow him off into the wilderness to meet a dozen more just like him."

"Then why did you ever agree to this?"

"He's a connection with Daniel, and he might remember more about their meeting."

As they approached a cluster of buildings on the right side of the road painted an improbable shade of pink, Trig swung off the highway and into the blacktop parking lot in front of the buildings. At least twenty motorcycles of all types were lined up in front of a dozen small cottages that formed a U behind a building marked "office."

"The gang's all here," David said as he followed Trig.

Carin suddenly laughed and startled David. But he didn't have to ask her what was so funny. He could clearly see a ten-foot-high sign on top of the office that was lined with huge light bulbs that probably flashed at night.

"The No-Tell Motel," he read.

Chapter Ten

He pulled the BMW into a space in front of the office near Trig's bike, and as the biker got off and came over to David, he said, "I'll let Ike know we need to use another unit for a while." He grinned. "He's used to renting them by the hour, anyway." Then he disappeared into the office while the other bikes parked.

"The No-Tell Motel?" Carin said. "I thought that was a joke, not an actual place."

David turned to Carin as Scat came over to Carin's door and looked down at her. "Did you ever think about getting a tattoo?" he asked Carin in a high nasal voice. It was the first time David had heard the man speak.

Carin looked up at him. "No, I haven't."

"You should. I do a great job." He tapped the teardrop on his forehead, then turned and called out, "Gem?" The girl with him was doing something at the bike, but when he said her name, she hurried over to him. He pointed to the tattoo on her arm. "Did that, and..." He turned Gem around, then lifted the back of her vest to expose her waist. A very distinct ball and chain had been tattooed with red highlights around her waist.

"See that? Great work. Some of my best." He let go of the woman's vest and smiled, exposing crooked teeth. "Women are my specialty."

"Hey," Trig called, and David saw him coming out of the office. He tossed some keys to Scat, then tossed one to David. As David caught it, Trig said, "You and your old lady have the shack at the end. It's yours until morning."

He walked off toward Pec, and David looked down at the key with its green plastic tag stamped with the number ten. "One room," he murmured.

"And one shower," she said, color brushing her cheeks, but her smile was filled with fun. "First one there gets dibs," she said as she snatched the key out of his hand and scrambled out of the car.

She was halfway to the room before David was out and had his seat tipped forward. As he circled the car, he saw Carin was already at the last unit. She glanced back at him, held up the key, then turned to unlock the door. With a pleased smile she disappeared into the room.

He took his time going around to tip her seat forward and grab her purse off the floor. One room, one shower. As he approached the open door, he took the step in a single stride and went inside.

The unit was surprisingly nice, with pale pink walls, beige carpet and bleached wood furniture. And one very large bed.

David swung the door shut, heard the shower running behind a closed door at the far side of the room, and saw Carin's sandals discarded on the carpet by the bed. Her cap was hanging on the back of a wooden chair near a small vanity by the bathroom door.

One bed wouldn't make any difference, he thought. They'd shower, change into fresh clothes, then start east looking for the bars. He spotted the phone on the nightstand and crossed to sink down on the off-white bedspread as he reached for the receiver. He'd totally forgotten to try to call Daniel from the car.

While he determinedly ignored the sounds of Carin behind the bathroom door, he dialed Daniel's number in San Diego. After just two rings, the answering machine clicked on and Daniel's recording said, "If you called, it has to be important, so leave your name and number. We'll get together soon."

When the beep sounded, David had to swallow once before he could speak into the phone. "Daniel, it's me, David. If you're there, pick up. Please, pick up." He waited and nothing happened. "Daniel, I'm looking for you. I'm in Arizona now, with Trig, the biker from Hell's Way. If you get this message, stay by the phone. I'll call back later tonight."

Hope dies hard, he thought as he hung up, knowing he'd actually had a moment when he thought Daniel would answer the phone and get a laugh out of his twin's wild-goose chase. There wasn't any laughter now, but for all he knew, this was exactly that . . . a wild-goose chase. Lying back on the bed, he closed his eyes and laid his forearm over them.

He could hear the shower still going, feel the hardness of the mattress under him, and inhale that peculiar odor that all motels seemed to have. He exhaled, and in the next heartbeat, deathlike cold surrounded him. He wasn't asleep. He knew that as surely as he knew that he was caught in a nightmare that had nothing to do with the vulnerability of sleep.

Yet he couldn't move. He couldn't open his eyes. He couldn't escape. Whatever was happening to him, whatever was possessing him, didn't need the cover of sleep to materialize. And he had no power to stop it or run from it.

Cold everywhere, isolation. A touch, but as insubstantial as a feather on his face. Pain in his chest, deep, wrenching pain. Air being pushed into his lungs, being sucked out. Fire in his throat. Pain like bolts of lightning searing through his legs and arms.

Weakness engulfed him. There was no strength left in him. He wanted to rest, to leave it all behind. Breathing was too much for him. There was nothing left in him to keep going. No strength to keep living.

Dying. He felt it. He felt the loss of life in his feet and hands, then his legs and arms. Dying. And, God help him, it wasn't a dream.

He could still hear the shower, feel the bed, the weight of his arm on his eyes, yet he was dying. Giving up. *No,* he wanted to scream. There was no way he could give up. He had to fight it, he thought. *Fight it! Don't give in. Don't let it happen. Not now. Not now. Breath, absorb the pain, let it go. Let it take on its own life so you can live yourself.*

Fight! Fight! Don't go easily. Don't let it happen. Don't let it take you. Don't! Don't. And his life was mixed up in a blur, until he suddenly was focusing past the terror, and the one thing he could sense clearly was Carin. Dying now wasn't possible. Not now. Not when he'd just found her.

That thought was as jarring as the horror that surrounded him, and he heard himself moan. He couldn't
give up. Not now. Not now. And without warning, he
was out of it. He was in the motel, in every sense of the
word. Whatever had happened, had stopped as suddenly as it had begun. He took his arm off his eyes,
and stared at the ceiling, taking in ragged breaths.
He'd stopped something, but he had no idea what.

He heard the door open and he knew Carin was
coming into the room. And in that moment, the one
thing he wanted to see, no, he needed to see, was her.
When she came to the bed, when he looked up and she
was there, he remembered the thought in the nightmare. He'd just found her.

The sight of her made thoughts of death flee. They
slid away slowly out of his consciousness, taking the
pain and terror with them. She was over him, in nothing but a white towel, her hair damp from the shower,
and tiny ringlets clung to her scrubbed face.

And in that moment, the world centered into a sanity that he'd never known existed, a sanity that over-
ruled the terror of moments ago. And that sanity was
Carin. She was the sum total of his world, of his existence, and the idea felt so right that it scared him.

A woman who was everything he wasn't, who had
a mystical way of looking at things, a woman who was
obsessed with the idea of twins. And all he could think
of was he was obsessed with her.

"David?" she whispered as he looked at her.

"I've made a terrible mistake," he said, not moving.

She frowned, her delicate brow furrowed. "What
mistake?"

"I apologized for what happened at the canyon this morning."

She shook her head. "I don't—"

David sat up and reached out to her, taking her hands in his. They felt small and delicate, and cool from the shower. "I should have never apologized for doing what I've wanted to do ever since you walked into that boathouse."

She smiled suddenly, a radiant expression that made his heart lurch. "Then I won't accept the apology," she breathed and moved closer to him.

He tried to smile, but when she leaned down to touch her lips to his, the expression faltered. She was sanity and insanity all in one incredible package. And he pulled her down onto the bed with him, back onto the mussed bedspread, and she laughed, a sound of pure pleasure. The next moment, she was in his arms. Her skin was like silk under his hands, the soft warmth of her a balm to his nerves, and when she came to him, everything else was shut out.

It didn't matter that she was as different from him as night from day, or if he said something was white, she'd say it was black. His mouth found hers, soft and yielding, and the only truth that mattered was the truth of the depth of his feelings for her. Ever since he'd found her at the door to Daniel's home, she'd begun to take over his soul. He knew that now. As his tongue tasted her, and his hands pushed aside the towel she was wearing, he had the shattering knowledge that she was becoming part of his soul.

He shifted her, needing to see her, to know she was real and not the product of another dream. As his hand touched her cheek, he found himself looking into

her blue eyes, eyes that seemed to echo the intensity in
him. The ball of his thumb skimmed over her full
bottom lip. He saw it tremble. "My God, I feel as if
I've been waiting for this forever," he breathed, his
voice hoarse with desire as he spoke a truth he hadn't
known existed until he said it.

He trailed his hand to her shoulder, then moved
back enough to see her. He wanted her fully and completely and he wanted this to last forever. He didn't
want to rush, to have it over before it could really begin, but as he looked at her high full breasts with their
rosy peaks already tightening provocatively, it literally took his breath away. Tentatively he lowered his
hand and found the silky heat, and as he cupped the
weight of her breast, he felt Carin tremble.

When his mouth took the place of his hand, when
he covered her nipple with his lips and drew it into his
mouth, she moaned and arched toward him. He felt
her hips pressing against his and he slid his hand down
to cup the sweep of her waist, to draw her even closer
to him. When she felt his arousal against her, she
moaned again and tugged at his shirt.

"Take it off," she moaned, her hands working
awkwardly to undo the buttons.

David moved back a bit and quickly took off his
shirt as her hands fumbled with the button of his
jeans. She tugged, unsnapped them, then helped him
push them down and free his legs. The next moment,
she was against him again, skin to skin, heat to heat,
and what he'd intended to do with control, to enjoy
for as long as he could, fragmented.

Her desire matched his, and each person explored
the other, hands and tongues, finding places that made

breathing stop or produced low moans. Words were everywhere, soft, urgent words lost in the intensity of the need of each person. And David felt lost, but there wasn't any fear. It was a completion that he'd never known existed until now, but he wanted it desperately.

Carin skimmed her hands over him, teasing him, finding him, circling him as his desire grew into an exquisite agony. If he could have surrounded her and pulled her into his being, he would have. He would have linked himself with her irrevocably, and as her hand stroked him, as her lips tasted his skin, as her tongue teased his nipple, he groaned.

He covered her hand with his, not ready to let the sensations take over. And when she stilled, he touched her, found her center and felt the moistness that invited him to join with her. She whispered, "Yes, oh David, yes," as he slowly moved his hand on her. Her head arched back, and he looked down at her, at her closed eyes, the flush of pleasure on her cheeks, and her tongue barely touching her lips.

He moved faster, felt her press to his touch, and he found her breast. The combination of sensations made her cry out. Every other experience in his life paled. This was what his life had been all about from the start. Carin, finding her and making love with her.

Then her eyes opened, the blue filled with desire, and she drew his hand away from her body and laced her fingers with his. "I want you," she whispered. "Love me."

And he moved without hesitation. He shifted until he was over her, his strength testing her, then as her legs came up and circled his waist, he filled her.

Slowly, he slipped into her until he was deep in the velvet moistness. And for a moment he hesitated, letting ripples of pleasure subside just a bit before he began to move.

She moved with him, matching thrust for thrust, her fingers digging into his shoulders, her rapid, shallow breathing an echo of his own. The feeling grew and grew, spreading through every atom of his body, filling every void, pleasuring every place that had hurt before. His ecstasy seemed to know no bounds. With each stroke it went higher and higher, and just when he thought he could touch her soul, the sensations exploded in him. He called out her name, and as she came in a shuddering cry, he felt her spasm around him, adding to his own climax. For that moment in time, he was lost. Then he felt her and knew the beauty of complete surrender to another person. What she'd said had been true. He'd always held back a part of himself that he protected and hid from others.

But not now. He simply let go.

Waves and waves of joy surged through him, shimmering, fiery pleasure that went on for what seemed forever. Then ever so slowly, he tumbled back to reality. And reality was Carin under him, him still in her, and a world that would never be the same again.

With a wrenching regret, he left her, and moved onto his side, but he didn't let go of her. He circled her with his arm and pulled her tightly to his side. If he had his way, he'd never let go of her again.

Logic and rational thought had no place in the world Carin discovered with David. All that belonged was feeling and sensations. As David held her, she felt a desire in her that was even stronger than before they had made love. She touched her lips to his chest and felt his breathing catch. He tasted of salt and heat and maleness. It was a heady combination.

She touched his stomach and felt the sweat on his skin. When she moved her hand lower, he exhaled in a rush. Would her need for him ever be satisfied? She tried to get closer, wishing she could melt into him and become a part of him.

David turned, and when she saw his eyes, she knew he felt the same way. Without a word, he took her again, slowly and completely, as she lifted her hips to him. She needed him in a way that seemed as elemental as breathing itself.

When he filled her, when she felt his strength touch her core, she gasped from the joy of it. Over and over again, she met him, going higher and higher until the world was gone. All that remained was David and her. When the moment came, she cried out as spasms of wonderment shook the foundations of her existence and as she held onto David, she knew the true meaning of two becoming one.

WHEN CARIN STIRRED from a deep, dreamless sleep, she reached out for David, but found the bed empty beside her. The wrench of not feeling her body against his threw off the rest of her sleepiness. She raised herself on one elbow to look around the room. With the drapes still drawn, the room was dim, vaguely touched by shadows.

She had no idea what time it was, or how long she'd slept with David. Pressing her free hand to the pillow by her that still held the imprint of his head, she felt the coolness of the linen. He'd been gone long enough for the bed to become cold, but her body still remembered him. Her breasts felt tender, and a vague throbbing deep inside only validated the fact that she could never get enough of him.

"Carin?"

The sound of him saying her name made her turn and she saw him in the doorway to the bathroom. The steam from a shower hung in the room behind him. His damp hair clung at his temples and neck, and he was wearing only a towel at his lean hips. No, she'd never get enough of him. Just the sight of his bare chest, the pattern of dark hair that disappeared into the towel, the strength of his legs and shoulders made her whole body respond with such intensity that she could barely breathe.

When she'd come into the room earlier after her shower, he'd been so still on the bed. Then he looked up at her, and everything had just fallen into place. When she'd come into the room, she'd had the feeling that something was wrong, but that thought fled when he reached out to her.

"Why didn't you sleep?"

"I couldn't," he said without coming closer.

"Why can't you sleep?"

He stayed very still. "I don't know."

"Were you asleep before?"

"No."

She felt as if he was shutting her out, and it made a pain in her heart that she couldn't begin to define. "Can't you tell me what's going on?"

"I don't know myself," he said in a low voice.

"David..." She nibbled on her bottom lip. Her desire to help him was staggering, but the vulnerability she'd seen when they'd made love wasn't there now. And she was terrified if she let it go, she'd never see it again. "The nightmares you have—"

"They're nothing," he said, yet she knew that they were probably everything to him. She could feel the barrier between them growing. For the first time since he had taken off her towel and she'd lain naked before him, she felt embarrassment. The sheet had fallen to her waist and her breasts were exposed, and she felt uncertain about so many things now, she found herself fumbling to tug the sheet up to cover herself.

"Don't," David said, his voice low and hoarse.

Her hand stilled, and Carin met his gaze. Even across the room, she felt the impact of his need, a need that echoed deep inside her. *Talk about living on the edge,* she thought as fire began to build in her. She'd tumbled over the edge into a place she had never been before, a place where David was everything, and nothing else mattered.

She loved him. The thought came in a beat of her heart, and she let go of the sheet. As it slipped down, she knew this love didn't make sense. It didn't have any logic. Not any more than the fact that she knew she'd never truly loved any man before him. She'd liked some, even cared about some, but never truly loved a man before.

She sat very still, the simplicity of her feelings overwhelming. As David came to her, there were no doubts and an odd peacefulness surrounded her. It was that simple. As David stopped by the side of the bed and looked down at her, she slowly got to her knees.

The sheet slipped off of her completely, but she didn't hesitate. Almost on eye level with him, she reached out and touched him. With unsteady fingers, she traced the line of his jaw, feeling the bristling of a new beard that darkened his chin. "No razor," he breathed. "Everything's in the car."

"Not everything," she whispered as she skimmed over the roughness, then touched his lips with the tip of her finger. "Not everything," she repeated, and lifted her face to his.

His kiss was almost tentative at first, a light contact about as substantial as the brush of butterfly wings, as if they both knew that if the contact grew, they would have passed some invisible point of no return.

Fire exploded in Carin as his tongue grazed her teeth, and her arms went around his neck. Her bare breasts pressed to his chest, and she was in his embrace. The two of them tumbled back into the mussed linen of the bed, and the lovemaking this time was a gentle exploration of each other.

She tasted him, exploring him with her tongue and lips, and the essence of the man filled her, saturating her being. His hands knew her, as if they had had access to her for years, gliding over curves, finding spots that made her moan with pleasure. When the heel of his hand began to slowly rotate on her most sensitive spot, she arched toward him, letting waves of sensation wash over her again and again.

When she was certain she would never be able to feel anything more exquisite, he was over her, the angles of his body fitting hers as if they had been made for each other. And when he filled her, she knew that there were no boundaries to her feelings with him. Her pleasure was so intense that she just held onto him for a long moment, letting him settle in her, letting the feeling of being joined become a reality.

Then as he began to move, she felt frantic with need. She rocked her hips to meet his thrusts, wanting him deeper and deeper in her, as if she could physically break that last barrier. As if she could will David to be everything to her, to let her know him in every way possible, she held onto him, her fingers digging into his shoulders.

As pleasure exploded in her, as she climaxed with such exquisite intensity that she cried out from it, tears came. Even as David trembled, then found her mouth with his, the tears slipped from her eyes. Then he left her, drawing her against his side, her cheek pressed to the beat of his heart, and she tasted the saltiness of her own tears. His fingers smoothed her hair back from her forehead, then his arm circled her, holding her against him.

She closed her eyes, her fingers splayed on his stomach. With the damp heat of his skin against hers, she swallowed hard. Their bodies could touch, they could meld and join, yet she wanted to touch his soul.

She ran her tongue along her lips, tasting the saltiness of her own tears. "David?" she whispered.

"Mmm?" His fingers trailed along her bare arm.

"I need to—"

An ear-shattering pounding on the door echoed in the room and cut off her words. David shifted, looking toward the door, but he didn't let go of her.

"Yes?"

"It's me, Trig! Gotta talk to you."

David looked at Carin and with a fleeting touch of his finger to her cheeks, he frowned. "Tears?"

"Hey, you two stop whatever you're up to and open the door," Trig called.

Carin covered her hand with his and managed a smile. "I'm fine."

David hesitated, then quickly kissed her forehead and rolled away from her to get out of bed. For a moment she saw him with a clarity that was almost painful. The muscularity of his back, the strength in his legs. Her heart contracted. She'd never dreamed that love could do this to a person, that it would make you see everything differently, that the person you loved could stamp images in your mind that would last for a lifetime and beyond, and make you feel such sadness that it was a physical pain in your heart.

She watched him reach for his discarded slacks and step into them. As Carin sat up and tugged the sheets to cover herself, David glanced back at her, flashed her a smile that took her breath away, then opened the door.

Trig partially blocked the sunlight that Carin was surprised to find was low in the sky. She glanced at the bedside clock. It was just after four in the afternoon. As she glanced back at Trig, she caught his gaze on her and a smile showing above his beard. "I guess you and me riding off into the sunset just isn't going to happen, is it, beautiful?"

"No, it's not," she said, knowing her face was flooding with color.

"Maybe in another life," the man said, then looked at David. "Before I left, I wanted to check and make sure I gave you a bar just outside Barryville, about forty miles this side of Demming on the way to Las Cruces."

"What was it?"

"Marty's Machine."

"I don't remember if it's on the list."

"Thought I'd tell you because I remembered telling your brother about the owner who's got a vintage Harley on display. The machine is cherry. One of the first in the state. T. J. said he wanted to make sure to see it either coming or going."

"I appreciate you stopping by to tell me."

"When you find him, tell him Trig and Hell's Way'll be looking for him at Shadow Canyon one of these days."

"I will." David glanced back at Carin. "I'll walk out with him and get our bags. I'll be right back."

Trig looked over at Carin and didn't move for a minute. "If you ever get over your phobias about bikes, get in touch."

"I will," she said.

Trig winked at her, then turned, and without a look back, David went with him, closing the door behind the two of them.

Carin sank back in the bed, combing her tangled hair back off her face with her fingers, then drew her legs to her breasts and pressed her forehead to her knees. Years of education and internship and she didn't have a clue about how to help David.

Abruptly, she got out of bed and headed for the bathroom. The room was still a bit steamy from David's shower and for a moment she thought she could catch a hint of his scent in the warm air. A towel had been tossed onto the sink, and she picked it up. She held the damp terry cloth to her breasts, to the tender fullness that was still there from their lovemaking. She wished that she could hold David again and again and again. Until she understood everything about him.

Foolish, she told herself and tossed the towel back onto the sink before she crossed to the shower, turned on the hot water, and stepped under the stinging spray.

DAVID CAME BACK into the room with the luggage and Carin's briefcase. He heard the shower going, and he crossed to the bed, setting the bags on the mussed linen along with the briefcase. He opened his bag, took out fresh clothes and dressed quickly in jeans and a plain white shirt. He fingered his jaw and felt the bristle of a beard. When Carin came out, he'd shave.

He sank down on the side of the bed and as he touched the sheets, he could have sworn he could still feel the heat of both of their bodies caught in the material. He'd never experienced what he had with Carin with any other woman who had come in and out of his life. Nothing even close. And he knew that he never would again.

Life was strange. Daniel disappeared. Carin appeared. She'd offered to come with him to find his brother, and from the first, he'd thought he'd made a mistake. The only mistake he'd made was fighting her when she'd offered to come with him. Right now, he knew that he'd have pushed away his one chance to be happy if he'd won out at the houseboat.

He leaned against the headboard and started to close his eyes, then stopped. Sitting up straight again, he knew he couldn't deal with another nightmare, awake or asleep. Right then, he knew that when Carin had offered to let him talk about what was happening, he should have taken her up on it. There had to be some way to make sense out of it and stop it.

Sleep was his enemy now, and when Carin had slept before, he'd lain there, not closing his eyes, but just watching her, envying her ability to sleep. He'd lost that as surely as he'd found her.

"We're losing him," he heard someone say, but he knew he was alone. No one was here. The shower was still going. Then he froze. The voice was in his mind, a man, at a distance, down a tunnel, but as real as the sounds of the shower. "We're losing him."

David stood, but the sounds that had nothing to do with his room didn't stop. A whooshing, a thump, a hissing, one, two, three. Then a bolt of fire shot through him. He fell backward onto the bed, his legs and arms tingling horribly. Another bolt of fire. Whoosh, thump, hiss. God, he couldn't stop it. Another bolt of fire.

"We're losing him!"

Chapter Eleven

David was on his back in the motel room staring at the ceiling, but he wasn't there.

He was lost, feeling things, but seeing only reality. Then it was gone, as suddenly as it had come, and he was breathing as if he'd run a marathon. Dammit. He sat up and rubbed his arms harshly, as if it would kill the tingling. He decided he'd talk to Carin, tell her what had been happening and see if she could make sense out of it.

The shower stopped, and as he turned he accidently knocked Carin's briefcase onto the carpet. It hit with a thud and the three-ringed notebook inside flipped open, scattering pages everywhere.

He quickly got off the bed and crouched to pick up the mess. But as he reached for the nearest page filled with Carin's writing, he felt his world explode. The date at the top of the entry was two days ago.

The second subject, to be known as T-12, doesn't appear to trust anyone, vastly different from T-11. It will take a great deal of work to get him to open up so the possibilities of psychic bonding can be explored thoroughly. If T-11 has disappeared, can T-12 sense it? Can it be factoring into his decisions?

David scanned the rest of the page and another sentence leapt out at him.

To have a firsthand chance to observe the possibility of psychic connection in the search for subject T-11 is unprecedented. T-12 has agreed to let the observer go with him on the search. Can psychic bonding can be experienced one-way? Can there be links that have a single path? Can that be the reason that T-11 has experienced no interlinking with T-12?

He closed his eyes, then reached for the pages, pushing them together. Tossing them on the bed, he turned and picked up the binder. Much the same way someone keeps testing an aching tooth, David turned back to the paper on the bed. One dated yesterday, was on the top now.

It now appears T-12 is hypersensitive to T-11. Paths that were undefined have been vividly recognized by T-12. Hell's Way, not the place geographically first thought, is a group of people. Yet T-12 not only found the group, he found an out-of-the-way canyon where the people congregated, and where T-11 has been. A single coin in an area of several acres was the lead to physical evidence T-11 had been there. T-12 seems to reject any hint of linking, but . . .

He fought the urge to tear up the pages as he read another page.

It is imperative to win the trust of T-12. There is something going on that is being held back, and whatever it takes, it must be discovered. T-12 closes off the response—

"David?"

It startled him to hear Carin say his name, and as he stood back from the bed, he looked up. Carin was in the doorway to the bathroom; her image was painfully beautiful to him. Her hair was tumbled around her, the towel used as a sarong, and her eyes looked huge. So beautiful and so driven, he thought, willing to do "whatever it takes" to give her investors in her study their money's worth.

She came toward him. "I need to talk to you and..." Her voice trailed off when she saw the mess on the bed. She looked back at David.

He met her gaze, wide with questions, and he had to swallow bitter sickness to be able to speak at all. "I'm subject T-12. Why humanize this whole thing by using my name?"

She clutched the towel at the front, her knuckles white. "What are you—"

He picked up a handful of papers and tossed them into the air. As they drifted down onto the bed, he took a step back, building more space between himself and this woman, hoping it would help ease his sense of being used, a sense tinged with the sting of betrayal. "Your damned study, Dr. Walker, with subjects T-11 and T-12."

"You were going through my notes?"

"No, I dropped your briefcase and the notes scattered all over the place." He pushed his hands into his pockets, needing to control the urge to grab Carin by her shoulders and shake her until he felt better. "'The second subject, to be known as T-12, doesn't appear to trust anyone.' Your own words." He took a harsh breath. "'It's imperative to win the trust of T-12, to do whatever it takes.'"

"David, you've taken it all out of context."

He turned his back on her and began to button his shirt, annoyed that his fingers were unsteady. "Up close and personal," he muttered, then dropped down on the bed and reached for his shoes and socks. "Get into bed with T-12, get him involved, get close, maybe he'll spill his guts."

He knew she was moving toward him. As much as he hated it, he could smell her freshness and heat in the air. As he pushed his foot into his shoe, her bare feet were not more than two feet from him.

He looked up, shocked at the reaction of his body just at the sight of her. "Listen to me, please," she said.

"No, you listen to me." He stood, thankful that he was towering over her. "T-12 was just about to spill his guts to you. Ironic, isn't it? I'd just decided to explain some things to you, and now—" He raked his fingers through his hair, hating the way she was looking at him, as if *he* was hurting *her*.

"I'm sorry. I . . . I never thought that—"

"Oh, you *did* think. You were thinking all the time," he muttered as he moved past her, making very sure not to touch her. He headed for the door, but she stopped him by hurrying after him and grabbing him by his forearm.

He stopped and stared down at her hand on his arm. Then he met her gaze. The pain was his, not hers. No matter what he thought he saw there. "David, you don't understand."

He pulled away from her touch. "What don't I understand?"

"You don't really think I went to bed with you just to find out something for the study, do you?"

He closed his eyes for a moment, her words cutting as deep as any knife could. Then he met her gaze. "I don't know. Maybe it's another crazy idea of yours, like the detective was, or whatever the other fiancé's name was. I don't know anything about you."

She took a breath, and he could see the shudder on the intake of air. Then she asked in a low voice, "What are you going to do now?"

"Go to the bars. Find Daniel."

"By yourself?"

"By myself."

Carin looked at David, and the total absence of emotion in his face and voice was making her cold. "But you don't have a car."

"I'll get one."

She knew there wasn't a thing she could say right now that would make any difference at all. But he needed a car. "All right," she said. "The BMW's yours. You've got the keys."

He stared at her. "What?"

"Take it. Go and find Daniel. I wish you luck."

He didn't move. "What about you?"

She swallowed the bitterness on her tongue. "I can call for a rental."

"No, I'll get a rental car." He turned from her and she bit her lip hard to keep tears that were stinging the back of her eyes from falling.

She watched him go to the phone, ring the desk and ask if the clerk could find a rental car for him. When he put down the receiver, he didn't look back at Carin. It was as if she was invisible.

Without a word, he repacked his bag, then began to stack her scattered papers. She couldn't bare to see him like this, so she made herself get her suitcase, then without looking at him, headed for the bathroom and went inside. Once the door was closed, she sank back against it and let her bag fall to the tile floor with a thud.

How could everything fall apart so completely in such a short time? "Physician, heal thyself," she muttered and swiped angrily at her tears. Quickly she dressed in navy shorts and a white T-shirt. She fastened her hair with a silver clip.

When she finally faced herself in the mirror, she was shocked to see how pale she was. Her eyes looked shadowed and wary, and her mouth was thin and tight. The sound of the phone ringing in the next room made her jump, and she quickly closed her suitcase.

When she went back into the bedroom, she saw David put down the phone with so much force that the sound of plastic striking plastic rang in the air.

"What's wrong?" she asked.

He didn't turn, but spoke as he stared down at the phone and pushed his hands into the pockets of his jeans. "The earliest they can get a car out here is to-morrow sometime . . . maybe."

"I told you, you can have my car."

"I told you, there won't be a car available until to-morrow sometime, if then."

"Then I'll stay here."

"You can't." He turned and reached for his bag, then he finally looked at her. And she wished he hadn't.

The cutting gaze from his hazel eyes made her stomach turn. He hated her. After everything that had happened between them, he hated her. "Yes, I can," she breathed.

"No, we'll go east and find a rental car on the way. Then you can have your BMW, your study, and I'll get out of your life."

"Logical to the end, aren't you?" she muttered.

"Take it or leave it."

She looked at him, and knew that staying alone in this room where they'd been together wasn't even an option now. She couldn't bear it. "When do you want to leave?"

"Now."

Without a word, she grabbed her cap, purse and suitcase and headed for the door. The heat was still intense, even though the sun was beginning to set in the west. But Carin only took the time to put on her sunglasses before she walked to her car. She heard David coming up behind her, passing her, and open-ing the trunk and tossing his bag inside.

He came to where she was standing by her door and took the suitcase from her, his hand never touching hers. He thrust her briefcase toward her. "You'll have to straighten out your notes. I just shoved them inside." Then he put her bag in the trunk and went around to get behind the wheel.

Carin opened the door, tugged her seat back, then slipped on to the leather. Before she even had the door closed, David had the car started and in gear. "Do me a favor?" he said as he drove out onto the highway again.

She was almost afraid to ask him what he needed. And she didn't have to. He kept talking, obviously his question rhetorical.

"Check out this page with the bars on it." He handed her the folded paper. "See if Marty's Machine's on the list."

She settled in the seat and scanned the page, holding it back a bit so she wouldn't need her glasses. David's handwriting was remarkably like Daniel's. She skimmed the list. "It's not here," she said, surprised that her voice sounded so normal and composed.

"Write it down. Trig said it's outside of Barryville, this side of Demming."

She found a pen in her purse, scribbled down his words under his writing on the list, then folded it and held it out to him. "Here."

He glanced at it, but didn't take it. "What's the first bar Trig said we'd hit on this road?"

She pulled the paper back and opened it again. "The Pit. It's probably sixty miles east of here."

He didn't say anything else, so she folded the paper again, tucked it in the console with his unfinished granola, then opened her briefcase. The papers had been shoved inside and the binder was under them.

Methodically, she put the papers in order, then snapped the rings and closed the notebook. She'd never dreamed David would see these, or if he did that he'd react so violently to her putting down thoughts about his relationship with his brother. But she should have known. David never wanted anyone to intrude on the part of him that was hidden. And she'd come so close. He hated her for it.

She closed the briefcase and tossed it into the back. She stared out at the landscape, flat bottomland and buttes scattered on the horizon, all shimmering in a heat that was lessening very little as night approached. "You know that there isn't going to be any car rental agencies open after five or six o'clock."

"Then we'll keep driving until morning," he said.

Carin didn't look at David. Instead, she closed her eyes and rested her cheek against the seat, then hugged herself, pressing her fingers into her upper arms. She had never felt this alone before in her life, not even when she was driving by herself to Albuquerque. She'd lost a part of herself that she'd barely even had time to understand.

David had driven for about an hour before he glanced at the gas gauge and saw it was just above empty. The road they were on was all but deserted, with oncoming cars few and far between. For the past ten minutes, they had been the only car heading east on this road.

Buttes rose out of the flatlands, and off in the distance, a purple blur of the coming night, he could make out what looked like mountains. He wished he'd thought of gas when he left the motel, but his mind had been almost shut down then. All he'd wanted was to get out of there and do something besides having to look at Carin or hear her talk or be in a closed place with her.

Hell, he hadn't thought of much for the past hour except what had happened with Carin. No matter how much pain there was, he couldn't quite get past the wrenching memory of her in his arms, the flush of passion on her face, the trembling when he touched her.

Life was an incredible joke. Things were illusions. Carin certainly had been until an hour ago. For the first time since they'd left the motel, he glanced at her. She was asleep, her head lolled to the right, her sunglasses on her lap and one foot tucked under her. The cap shaded her face a bit, but even in the failing light of coming evening, he could see the dark arch of her lashes on her cheek, and the way a pulse beat at the hollow of her throat.

She looked vulnerable and beautiful, her skin smooth and delicate. His response at the sight of her undermined every logical fact that he knew. He looked away to the road ahead and thankfully spotted a faded sign offering Gas and Food, 5 Miles Ahead.

He pressed the accelerator, speeding up, and as he spotted a glow in the night ahead, the cold came. He knew from the first instant what was happening, and he instinctively hit the brakes. But even as the car squealed to a stop on the dusty shoulder of the highway, David was in a place that both terrified and hurt him.

He began to shake uncontrollably, his hands clenched on the steering wheel, and even though he could see the world outside the car, he wasn't there.

He'd been thrown into another level, where cold ate at him, pain radiated into every part of his being, and suddenly there was a light so bright it blinded him.

"David!"

He knew Carin was screaming at him, that she had him by one arm, shaking him. But he couldn't move. He couldn't look at her. The light was everywhere and heat was coming, searing away the cold. He knew he was in the car, but he could feel himself sailing backward, thrown as if he weighed nothing.

"David! David! Listen to me!" Carin's voice cut into the horror, and he stopped dead. Everything stopped. There was nothing but the slight vibration of the idling car engine. Carin's grip on his arm bit into his flesh, and he realized she held his face, her fingers clasping his chin.

Then he saw her, more than few inches from his face, her eyes filled with shock and concern.

His breathing was rapid and shallow, and he could feel dampness on his skin. Carin moved back a bit, releasing her hold on his chin, but her grip on his arm stayed. "My God, what happened?" she asked.

He blinked rapidly, gasping for air, and he sank back in the seat. He was on the side of the road, at an angle with the nose of the car pointed toward a five-foot-deep drainage ditch not more than two yards from the front fender. If he'd stopped just a few feet farther...

"David?" Carin said softly, so close he could feel her against his arm, but he couldn't look at her. He stared up at the darkening sky. "Please, let me help. Tell me what's going on."

He exhaled, then ran an unsteady hand over his face. "You'll have to drive," he managed to say in a hoarse voice, then turned from her and got out of the car. He stood for a moment to get his bearings, to let his legs get steady and his heartbeat settle into a near normal rhythm. But as he started to go around the back of the car to get in the passenger seat, Carin came around to meet him.

She stood in his path, and he knew she wasn't about to move. "Get in the car," he said.

"Not until you explain why you almost killed us."

He looked around, then back to her navy eyes regarding him with unblinking intensity. "Get in the car, and I'll explain everything."

Without a word, she brushed past him, got in the car, and by the time he got in on the passenger side, she was behind the wheel looking at him. "All right. Explain."

He looked away from her and slammed the door, then rested his elbow on the frame and closed his eyes. "Come," he heard, and opened his eyes.

"What did you say?" he asked Carin.

She glanced at him. "Nothing. I was waiting for you to do what you said you'd do...explain."

The wind over the buttes was playing tricks on him. Everything was upside down and crazy. And maybe he was the craziest of all. "I've been having dreams."

She kept quiet, letting him find the right words. He hated the feeling of confessing to a doctor, but he knew he had no choice. It had gone beyond dreams, beyond visions. He'd almost killed them.

He stared out at the night. "The night-mares...they started in Mexico. I meant it when I told you I never dreamed. I never have, or at least I haven't remembered them. But I woke from the second one right before you arrived at Daniel's houseboat."

"What was the dream about?"

He let his head lean against the backrest, and he deliberately kept his eyes open, almost certain if he closed them, the dreams would be there. "Death."

"What about it?"

"I was dying. I knew it. I could feel it, then something jarred me, and I was awake."

"You had it again when I was there, didn't you?"

"Yes, but it changed a bit."

"How?"

He licked his lips, and realized he was clenching his hands in fists on his thighs. Deliberately, he forced his hands open and spread his fingers on the denim of his jeans. "I could hear people talking, saying I was going to die, that they were losing me. The cold was everywhere and pain . . . the pain was beyond anything I could describe."

She waited silently.

"Then at the canyon, it happened again."

"The same?"

"Sort of, but I knew I had to fight. Someone was telling me something, I don't remember what, but I knew I could almost let go and die. But someone wouldn't let me. Then at the motel . . ." His hands clenched and he didn't even try to relax them. Maybe the way his nails bit into his palms could be a distraction, keep the visions from coming up on him again.

"What happened?"

"I wasn't asleep. I was awake. I knew I was awake, but it happened. The same cold and pain, and dying.

But I wasn't sleeping. I grabbed at life. I fought it, then you..." He took an unsteady breath. "And it happened again before we left."

"And when you were driving?"

"Yes. From nowhere, cold, pain, pressure on my chest. But it's not my chest. I don't think it is. But it's so real, so horrifying. It's like blacking out, only I knew I was in the car, that I was pushing the brake, but I couldn't stop what was happening."

"I knew someone who had the same sort of thing happen to them," she said.

"And you committed them?" he asked, trying to joke, but failing miserably.

"No. They weren't crazy. They were just feeling what someone else was really experiencing."

"Oh, God," he groaned.

"Don't do that."

"What?"

"Don't cut me off without hearing me out. Just let me tell you what I think, give me a chance, then you can have me committed if you want to or believe what I say."

"You've got a captive audience," he muttered.

"Exactly." She put the car in gear, then backed onto the road. As she headed east, she began to talk. "This person had an identical twin. One twin lived over a thousand miles from the other. They saw each other when they could, but they weren't inseparable. They had their own lives. Sort of like you and Daniel.

"Then one day for no reason, one twin had a dream. It was horrendous. There was a horrible accident, ripping steel, screaming people, but there weren't any visuals. Just the sounds. Just the feelings."

David felt his nails pressing into his palms, but he kept silent and stared straight ahead.

"For three days the dreams came, until the twin who was dreaming knew that something was wrong with the other twin. I don't know how the knowledge came, but it did. But when the twin tried to contact the other twin, there wasn't any answer, just a machine. Then the dream came, but it wasn't during sleeping. It was in the middle of the twin's living room. And there were screams, horror that couldn't be described, sinking and falling and terror."

Carin spoke quickly, words falling over words, and when David finally looked at her, she was rubbing her arm with one hand, back and forth, back and forth, quickly, almost as quickly as she was speaking. "Do you know what it was?" she asked.

"What?"

"The other twin was on an airplane flying to New York, and the plane was in terrible trouble. One of the engines exploded, caught on fire, and the plane lost altitude so rapidly that the oxygen masks were deployed. Just before the plane went into a fatal dive, the pilot got it under control and was able to land. There were more problems, foam was laid out for it, but the plane managed to land. No one was hurt."

"You're trying to tell me that the one twin experienced the other twin's nearly fatal plane trip?"

"Yes."

"You believe that?"

"I do." She never looked away from the highway, but David could see the way her jaw was clenched. "It happened. The twin was separated from the other twin by almost the whole country, but went through the physical sensations and terror that the other one did.''

David looked away from Carin, and he knew exactly where this was going. But before he could denounce it, before he could tell her she was crazy, he knew the truth. It came in a flash of understanding that shattered everything he'd believed up until then. Just the way finding out about Carin had shattered him.

He sat forward with his hand pressed to his chest. He could barely get out the question. "Daniel's dying, isn't he?"

Chapter Twelve

Carin slowed the car and glanced at David for the first time since she'd started talking. Why had she told him all of that? Had she known all along he was going through the same thing, or had it been a lucky guess?

"I didn't say he was dying," she said as David shook his head.

"My God, you were right. I can't believe I didn't realize it before."

"David, I was just giving you one possible explanation, that's all."

He looked at her, and the pain in his eyes ripped at her heart. "The only explanation."

"You might think this world is made up of absolutes, but I'm here to tell you it's not. You could just be having the dreams because of your worry about Daniel. The human mind—"

"Can't you forget you're a doctor for once?" he shouted out, anger tightening his expression.

She'd done that very thing at the motel, and she'd lived to regret it. She wasn't going to do that now. "I'm telling you facts. You can perceive things any way you want to."

"How about the twins you told me about? Did one twin just *think* there was a near plane crash, or *was* there a near plane crash?"

"Everything I told you was the truth."

"Then I need to find Daniel as soon as I can. I never thought I'd say this, but if I don't get to Daniel, he's going to die. That's the dying that Rick was talking about. Dying coming down big-time."

She didn't question the statement. She simply nodded. "I understand."

"I thought you would." He sat back in the car seat and his rough chuckle held no humor at all. "This'll make one hell of a case study for your notes, won't it?"

"I told you, I won't use any of it."

"I'm telling you, you will. You have to justify all the money you're getting from your backers. You'll give them exactly what they want."

She flinched at the tone of his voice. "You believe that?"

"I know that," he muttered.

Carin pressed the accelerator, anxious to get to where there was light and the night wasn't so encompassing. "I told you before that I wasn't perfect, but I really don't lie."

"You just omit the truth."

She felt sick, and couldn't think of a thing to say to him. Everything had changed so drastically in the past few hours, she wished she could turn back time. Swallowing, she felt her stomach lurch and remembered that she hadn't eaten since the trail mix snack last night.

"The truth is I wish I could take you right to Daniel, but I can't."

"But you think *I* could if I tried?"

She listened for sarcasm in his tone, but didn't find any, just intensity. "What do you think?"

He was silent for so long she thought he was ignoring her, then he shifted in the seat. "We need gas." He motioned ahead at a station to the right. "I think that's our last chance."

She drove in silence, swung into the gas station, got the tank filled and she didn't talk again until they were back on the highway. "What are you going to do?"

He exhaled in a harsh rush. "Tell me how I can make one of these visions, or whatever you want to call them, happen?"

She glanced at David, the night hiding most of his expression from her. But she could feel the tension in him. "What brought them on before?"

"At first it was sleeping, then just closing my eyes. The last time I was driving, wide awake, my eyes open."

"And you could see everything while it was happening?"

"No, there was a light, something that almost blinded me, then I saw you. How did it happen with the twins you told me about?"

"Sleeping, then waking, then at the time of the airplane problems, standing in the living room and everything was gone, leaving just the other twin's experience. I guess you could call it a blackout."

Carin saw a glow in the sky ahead and knew they were approaching a more populated area. "How far do you think it is to the first bar Trig told you about?"

"We should almost be there. Santa Ynez is next, and it's on the far side of the town, by a truck stop."

As she drove toward the town, Carin asked, "Do you want some advice? If not, just say so, and I'll keep quiet."

"Just say it."

"Let it happen. Just do what you're doing, and let it happen. And when it does, don't fight it. Experience it. Maybe we can figure out what's going on around Daniel, if you really are living his experience."

David didn't agree or disagree. He fell silent as they drove into the town of Santa Ynez, a fairly large place with adobe buildings, Spanish tile roofs, and groups of small businesses lining the main street.

Carin slowed and caught a glimpse of David in the light from the old-fashioned street lamps. He was staring straight ahead. For a moment she thought he might be beginning what she called an experience, but when he slanted her a look, she knew he wasn't.

"The Pit," he said.

She slowed for a stop sign. "What?"

"The bar, it's called The Pit."

She drove ahead and out of town. When she hit the outskirts and the highway cut off into the night, she spotted their destination. "There it is," she said, pointing ahead of them to a huge, glowing red ball in the distance that sat on top of a thirty-foot pole and rotated slowly. The Pit was emblazoned on it in huge black letters.

She slowed and as she turned into the parking lot, she got a good look at The Pit. It looked like a huge packinghouse, with rough wooden walls, a steeply sloped shingled roof and an entrance porch that ran the length of the front of the building with plank steps leading up to it.

The parking lot was gravel, and it was close to full with pickup trucks and motorcycles. In the red glow from the overhead sign, she could see groups of people hanging around outside smoking and drinking beer from cans. Some were in western wear, some in biker outfits. And the heavy beat of country music vibrated in the balmy night air.

Carin pulled into the parking lot, getting as close to the front as she could, then turned off the motor. She ignored a drunk who wandered past and muttered, "Buy American, honey," then staggered off.

"Jerk," David muttered and opened his door.

When Carin got out on her side, David looked at her across the car. "You stay here. Put up the top and lock yourself inside. I won't be long."

"I'm not staying out here. What if you black out in there?"

David stared at Carin, wishing she was stupid and foolish and that she didn't make a lot of sense most of the time. "Let's go," he muttered and slammed the car door.

She hurried around to fall in step beside him as he headed for the entry. He fought the impulse to grab her hand and not let go as they neared the entry. So he went ahead of her a few steps and entered the club first.

The room was vast, with high-beamed ceilings and a large bar to the right with a live band pounding out country music. Ahead of them was a sunken dance floor filled with couples, and to the right clusters of small tables. Flashing multicolored lights glittered down on the smoke-filled room, and the din of voices and laughter melted into the heavy beat of the music.

David spotted pool tables beyond the bar where the bikers congregated. He turned to Carin. "Why don't you ask around at the bar, and I'll go see the group over by the pool tables." He took out one of Daniel's pictures from his shirt pocket and handed it to her. "You'll need this."

She took the picture, then headed for a seat at the far end of the bar while he went in the direction of the pool table.

But before David could get through the crush of people around the dance floor, someone grabbed his arm and spun him around. A lanky blond cowboy with a droopy mustache and beer-bleary eyes ground out an obscene name that David didn't have to hear to understand. And the next thing he knew, the man swung his fist right at his face.

Carin heard a sudden explosion of screams and shouts, and by the time she turned from talking to the bartender, all hell had broken loose in the room. Fist-fights had broken out, spilling into the dance floor, and a man who looked like someone who would ride with Trig smashed a chair over the head of a cowboy who had been pummeling another man.

The band kept playing, just picking up the volume, and the crash of a mirror shattered by a thrown plate mingled with the country song. Carin stayed against the bar, searching the room for David, but she couldn't see him anywhere. Then what looked like a squad of gorillas—six men dressed all in black, from jeans to T-shirts—waded into the commotion, grabbing men at random and literally picking them up to pull them away from the fighting.

When the scene began to clear and Carin finally saw David, she almost cried. He was standing, his hands raised in fists, with blood on his knuckles. But what she couldn't take her eyes off of was his face. There was an ugly gash on his left temple with blood oozing from the ragged tear, matting in his hair, running down his jaw and dripping onto his torn shirt. His left eye was a livid red and almost swollen shut.

"David! David!" she screamed, frantically pushing through the press of people that separated her from him. She couldn't take a full breath until she broke free of most of the crowd and saw David not more than five feet from her. A lanky man was helping ease David into a chair.

"David," she gasped as she hurried to where he was sitting.

He looked up at her. His one eye had almost closed completely and the welt on his cheek was an ugly red. She had to close her eyes for a moment before she crouched by his chair and held the wooden arm to keep herself from reaching out and holding onto him. Someone pushed a white towel at her, and she glanced up at one of the bouncers. "Soak up that blood," the man said. "I'll be back in a bit."

"Thank you," Carin said, then balled the towel up and gingerly touched David's gash with it.

He flinched at the contact. "Dammit, that hurts."

"I thought you said you couldn't fight," she said as she dabbed at the wound, thankful that the blood flow was slowing considerably.

David let his head rest against the back of the chair as he closed his eyes. "Didn't say I couldn't," he muttered through clenched teeth. "Just don't like to."

"What happened?"

Someone came up beside Carin, and as she glanced to her right, she saw the man who had helped David into the chair. He was cut from the same mold as Trig, with a pure biker look from the heavy boots to the leather headband and long, gray-streaked hair. "They blindsided him," the man said in a gravely voice.

"They?"

"Those jerks." He motioned beyond him with his thumb. "Stupid yahoos. Give them a beer and they think they're King Kong. Too bad they fight like girls."

Carin kept the pressure on the wound at David's temple, but looked past the man to a crowd about six feet away. She could see that two people were on the ground and others were huddled over them. Bloodstains on the wooden floor were being trampled under the rush of people grabbing towels and offering advice.

"Why did they start the fight?" she asked the man crouched by her.

David shifted, taking the towel from her to hold it himself against his temple. She looked at him, at the sheen of perspiration on his skin that was horribly pale. "Thanks for helping me," David said.

"Least I could do," the man said.

"Why did he take a swing at me?"

"Because he's a coward. Had to get in the first hit." The guy held up one hand. "You hang tight, and I'll see if I can get it for you."

"Get what?" Carin asked, but the man was too quick for her. He was already heading across to the crowd around the men. Carin looked back at David. "Get what?" she asked.

"I don't know. I don't even know why the guy came at me like that."

She grimaced at the way his eye was closing and getting deep color. Impulsively she touched his arm, and almost felt an electric shock at the contact. But she didn't withdraw. "Are you going to be all right?"

"I got a roaring headache and I think I must have broken every bone in my right hand, but you're the doctor. You tell me."

She tried to smile at the joke, but found the expression faltered when she saw the way the blood from his temple wound was soaking through the white terry towel. "You need to get to a hospital and get some stitches."

"Later. I don't have the time now."

The man came back and crouched down by Carin, but he looked at David. With a grin, he pulled something from behind his back and held it up to David. "Ripped it off his finger. Here you go."

Carin stared at a heavy silver ring she'd seen on Daniel's finger before, and she had no doubt it had torn David's skin at his temple. There was still some blood clinging to the partially raised diamond set in the silver. "Where did you get that?" she asked.

"Damn hillbilly, Jake, kept it. Sort of a trophy for him." He shook his head, his face grim. "Sorry about your wallet, but you'd already left when we found out the jerk had lifted it. He got out before we could stop him and disappeared until tonight. If you want to call the cops, I'll back you on it. Throw his butt in jail for a while."

"What are you talking about?" David asked.

"Yeah, after you beat his butt at poker, he couldn't take it. You left your ring on the table. He took it, and while you were both at the bar, he took your wallet."

David lifted his bloodied hand and took the ring, but his eyes stayed on the man. "When was I here before?"

The man frowned. "Don't you know when you were here, or did that hit to the head scatter your brains?"

"I wasn't here. My brother was, my twin brother."

The man was clearly puzzled, but before he could ask any more questions, Carin cut in. "When was his brother here?"

The man moved back a bit. "You're not T. J.?"

"I'm his twin, David. When was he here?"

"A while ago."

David struggled to sit up straight, gripping the arm of the chair with his damaged hand. "When?"

"A week ago, maybe a bit longer." The man frowned at David. "What's going on?"

"I need to find my brother. Where did he go from here?"

"He didn't tell me. He just said he was heading back. Didn't even say where *back* was. He'd been on the road for a while and he stayed around for a few hours when we got into a poker game. He cleaned us all out. There should have been a couple of hundred in that wallet."

"And he left without his wallet or any money?"

The man shrugged. "Looks that way. That's why I was expecting him to come back anytime. I've been watching for him ever since."

"You've been hanging out here waiting?"

"Hell no, I work here. I'm the head of security."

"What?" Carin asked. "You're in charge of security and you were in the middle of the fight?"

"Lady, I'm a cooler, the top bouncer. I take care of things, and fights are part of the job description."

"All in a day's work, Mr. . . . ?"

"The name's Ray Logan, but my friends call me Manta as in Manta Ray. They think it's a joke. I'm used to it."

Carin looked at David, but he was staring at the man. "So, you're Manta?"

"Yeah, that's me."

"Do you know a biker from the Hell's Way gang called Trig?"

"Sure. I've known Trig ever since we served together in 'Nam years back. He's the one who sent your brother by. Why're you looking for T. J.?"

"He's dropped out of sight." David looked past Manta at the crowd where the two men were being helped to their feet. "Do you think that guy could have done something to him?"

"No. Jake's a devout coward. That's why he lifted your brother's wallet instead of facing the man down and why he blindsided you." Manta stood. "But it can't hurt to ask the man a few questions."

He crossed to a blond cowboy who still looked as if he had no idea where he was. His face was distorted from a swollen lip, a gashed cheek and a huge lump on his forehead. Two bouncers supported him at each arm, but Carin didn't miss the way the man cringed as Manta approached him.

Carin turned to David. "Daniel was all right a week ago. That's encouraging."

David sank back in the chair, resting his head and closing his eyes. "He left without his wallet, and he would have been back for it, if he could have come back."

She couldn't argue with that. "So, what do we do now?"

"I don't think there's any reason to keep going. He's either here or he's back the way we came. I'll find a rental car and head back."

Carin felt as if a rug had been pulled out from under her. She'd known she was only going to be with David until he got a rental car, but until that moment, she hadn't really dealt with the idea of him leaving. She hadn't faced the fact that at some point very soon, she'd watch David drive away from her forever.

She closed her eyes tightly for a moment, then as she opened them, Manta came back and tugged a chair over near David. As he sat down and David looked at him, he said, "Jake left here, got drunk, probably on your brother's money after he tossed the wallet. That's about it."

"Is he telling the truth?" David asked.

"I'd bet on it. Like I said, he's a devout coward."

David rubbed his thumb over the pattern on the ring. "I appreciate your help."

"Wish I could tell you more, but there isn't any more."

David dropped the ring in the pocket of his torn shirt, then gripped both arms of the chair. But as he tried to stand, Carin could see the way his legs buckled and she caught him by the arm. Slowly he sank back down in the chair. "You have to get that head wound looked at," she said, then looked at Manta. "Where's the closest hospital?"

"They've got a clinic in Santa Ynez, but it's only open during the day. The only real hospital is in Freemont, about twenty miles north of Santa Ynez. Do you need a ride?"

"No, we've got a car outside," Carin said, "but I could use your help getting him out to it."

"Sure," Manta said, then turned and whistled over the general noise in the room. Two bouncers hurried over. "Help this guy out to his car." He looked back at David. "Hope you find T. J."

Carin watched the two men help David to his feet and support him as they headed for the door. And she knew right then that she wasn't going anywhere without David until they found Daniel. Then she'd deal with how she could leave a man she loved more with each passing moment.

BY THE TIME Carin drove into the parking lot of Freemont General Hospital just before midnight, David felt as if his head and eye had a life of their own. They throbbed in unison and he'd lost the ability to open his eye enough to see anything.

He held a fresh towel to his head, and he could feel the heat of blood already soaking through the cotton. As he shifted and looked at the hospital, a glass and steel structure that had been built in one giant curve and soared twenty stories into the clear night sky, he tried to fight the thoughts that had been bombarding him.

Logically, he knew that Daniel might be dead. Even without the dreams and horrors, if a man left a place with no money and no wallet and hadn't been seen for a week, the chances were that something had happened. What had Carin said about twins that died within hours of each other? He closed that thought off as she spoke for the first time since they left The Pit. "There it is."

He looked ahead of them and could see a well lit, glass-door entry with a bright white and black sign, Emergency Entrance. As she pulled into a parking space right near the doors and shut off the car, she said, "Wait here. I'll get help," and got out of the car.

But David wasn't about to sit and wait. He opened the door and carefully gripped it for leverage to get out. By the time he had steadied himself and his head stopped spinning, the emergency-room doors shot open and a nurse and an orderly pushing a wheelchair were hurrying toward him.

"They were expecting us," Carin said as the orderly helped David into the wheelchair, then took the towel off his wound. Quickly the nurse pressed a gauze pad to it, secured it with a strip of adhesive, then nodded to the orderly. "Let's go."

"We've gotten a few of the victims from The Pit's brawls before," the intern said as he began to push David toward the doors.

David heard the nurse talking to Carin, asking questions, and he knew the orderly was talking to him, but suddenly he couldn't hear anything but a steady drone. The glass doors that another orderly was holding open for them were clear enough, but he knew he wasn't looking at them right. They were distorted, as if he was lying on his back looking up at them as he sped past.

He tried to shake his head to clear the confusion, but the next thing he knew, they were inside, the odors of disinfectant and rubbing alcohol everywhere. Bright light made his head feel as if it would explode. He pressed a hand to the developing pain in his chest and leaned forward. The next thing he knew, he was being lifted. He saw Carin right over him, her face filled with concern.

"David, David? Is it happening again?"

He wanted to say, "Yes," but he couldn't form the word. The pain in his chest was now excruciating, almost doubling him over. Someone touched his shoulder, pressed him down on the hard surface. "Stay still. Head wounds can be tricky."

But it wasn't his head, it was his chest. Didn't they understand? He looked at Carin still by him. Didn't she know? She had to understand. She was coming closer, he could hear her. "What's happening? Can you tell me? David, tell me what's happening. Where are you?"

Why could he see her so clearly, yet he couldn't say a thing? She touched him on the cheek, her fingers cool and lingering, yet he couldn't move. "It's all right," she was saying, coming closer to him. "I understand. Just feel and remember. Feel and remember."

Then she was gone and he felt as if life had been denied him. "Feel and remember," echoed in him, and he let himself go.

With his eyes open, he saw nothing. He felt coldness and heaviness in his chest. Pain in his side, deep, piercing pain. Not sharp, but unending. A throbbing. Air in his lungs. In and out. Air. He wanted to gasp, to suck in his own air, but he couldn't. He had to wait for the air to come, then be pressed out. And he knew. A respirator. It was breathing for him.

But it wasn't him. It was Daniel. A respirator. Daniel.

"Don't move," someone was saying and he knew the person was talking to him. He opened his eyes and saw a gray-haired, dark-skinned man leaning over him. "Mr. Hart, I'm Dr. Pine. We'll fix you up in a few minutes. First, I need to know when was the last time you had a tetanus shot."

He blinked his good eye, trying to focus. "Last...last year."

"Good. Then you won't need another one."

David looked around, but he couldn't see Carin.

The doctor removed the makeshift bandage, swabbed the wound with something cool and astringent, then stood back. "That's quite a gash, more like a rip. You'll need about six stitches to close it. I'm not a plastic surgeon, but I'll make you look as good as possible."

"Just do what you have to," David murmured.

Dr. Pine moved out of David's sight, then came back with a small flashlight. Carefully he prodded at the tenderness around David's swollen eye, then gently pried it open enough to shine the light in it. The brightness made his head hurt even more.

"Ah, huh," the doctor murmured, then pushed the flashlight into the pocket of his white coat. "You're going to have one hell of a shiner tomorrow, but the swelling should go down in a day or two."

He reached for David's right hand, examined it silently, then the other hand and stood back. "I'll need X-rays to be sure, but I think your hands are just swollen, no broken bones. Do you have any questions?"

"How long is this going to take?"

"An hour to get you cleaned up, then a night of observation."

"I'm not staying here overnight."

"Mr. Hart, when there's been a head trauma, it's usual to keep the patient under observation for twenty-four hours."

"But a patient doesn't have to stay, does he?"

"No, but—"

"Please, just do what you need to do."

"All right, Mr. Hart, but I'll have to put it down on the chart that you refused observation."

"Fine, do it."

"All right. I'll be giving you a local anesthetic for the sutures, drops for your eyes, and antibiotic cream for the cuts and scrapes. I'll need a signed consent form, then we'll get to work." The doctor looked at someone beyond the table. "Get the forms for me as quickly as possible."

"Yes, Doctor," someone said, then the doctor was looking down at David again.

"You won't reconsider staying with us just for a few hours?"

"No, I can't. The lady who's with me, where is she?"

"She's outside. The fight wasn't over her, was it?"

David almost smiled at that, but his whole face hurt too much. "No."

"Well, she'd be worth fighting over," the doctor said, then looked up as someone came into the room. "Dr. Carr? I didn't expect you. Where's the nurse?"

"She got tied up with an emergency and she asked if I'd drop these in on my way back upstairs. She said you needed them right away."

At the moment David heard the voice behind him, he knew he was slipping back into the scattered world of sensations and feelings. The voice. He'd heard it before, but only in the dreams and visions. It had drifted in and out, talking about dying and loss, a soft, gentle voice filled with sadness and urgency.

Chapter Thirteen

"I appreciate it, Dr. Carr," Doctor Pine said. "Mr. Hart's in a hurry to get out of here."

David caught movement out of the corner of his good eye, then he was looking up at a face that matched the voice, a face he had never seen before, but a face that looked familiar to him. The woman was petite, about thirty years old, with a wispy cap of strawberry blond curls framing a delicate heart-shaped face. Deep brown eyes looked gentle behind round, gold-rimmed glasses.

"The nurse filled in what she could from the gentleman's friend outside, but she'll need blood type, allergies and inoculations."

With each passing heartbeat, David knew this wasn't a vision. He was wide awake seeing reality. The woman smiled in a vague, distracted sort of way at first, not really seeing him. When she finally looked directly at David, her eyes widened with shock. "Oh..." she breathed and the clipboard she'd been carrying began to slip slowly from her fingers. She caught it just before it would have fallen to the floor.

"Dr. Carr?" Dr. Pine said. "Sara? Is something wrong?"

"He..." She licked her lips. "No, nothing's wrong. It's just..."

David understood exactly what was going on. "Do you know me?" he asked.

She shook her head. "No, I don't. It's just I thought..." She shook her head, hugging the clipboard to her chest. "I'm sorry."

"You think I look like someone, don't you?" he asked.

She looked at Dr. Pine, then back to David. "It's just...you look like a man they brought in here about a week ago."

She turned to the doctor. "You remember the John Doe who'd been in a motorcycle accident on the highway south of here?"

"I remember something about it. You were the internist on that case, weren't you?"

"Yes."

Carin was suddenly next to David, her hand on his shoulder. Thankfully, he didn't have to ask the question that was burned in his mind. "I'm Dr. Walker," Carin said. "I'm with Mr. Hart. I heard you mention a patient of yours who looked like Mr. Hart?"

"It's hard to say with the damage done, but there's a real likeness."

Carin's touch on David tightened and he felt as if she was giving him strength to deal with the answer to her next question. "Doctor, what happened to your patient, your John Doe? Did he survive? Is he alive?"

"What's this all about?" Dr. Carr asked.

"We need to know what happened to the man."

She glanced at Dr. Pine, then back to Carin. "He was in an accident south of here. The driver behind him said it looked as if his motorcycle stalled, then shot forward. It went out of control, hit the lip of a drainage ditch and sent him flying. His chest hit the handlebars, broke four ribs, fractured his collarbone, and he sustained a major concussion."

"But did he survive?" Carin asked, her voice tight.

David held his breath as the doctor began to talk. "We almost lost him a couple of times to an infection, and we had to revive him. He had a punctured lung. But, amazingly, he's holding his own now."

Even as she said the words, David realized he'd known Daniel was alive all the time. He'd fought with him to live. He'd struggled with him to breathe. He reached up to cover Carin's hand with his, needing the direct contact.

"Where is he?" David asked.

Dr. Carr glanced down at him as if she'd forgotten he was there. "On the fifth floor, intensive care."

"Is he on a respirator?" David asked.

"Now, he is. He was on life supports, but went onto a respirator yesterday."

"I want to see him."

Dr. Pine cut in. "Mr. Hart, I don't know what's going on here, and I can't make you stay for observation, but I can insist that you don't go anywhere until you get that wound stitched up."

"That man's my brother. I have to see him."

"Your brother?" Dr. Carr asked.

"His twin," Carin said. "And David's been looking for Daniel for days. He thought he might be dead. And now he knows he's not, he needs to see him."

Dr. Carr held tightly to the clipboard. "Daniel Hart? That's his name?"

"Yes."

"When he came in he didn't have any ID and the police were going to take prints to try and trace him." She stared at David. "How did you know he was here?"

"I didn't," David admitted. "But I knew he was in trouble." He looked at Dr. Pine. "Would you just get me stitched up so I can get out of here and see him?"

"Sign the forms, then I'll get it done as quickly as possible and you can go up there."

David managed to grasp the pen the doctor offered him and scrawl his name on the bottom of two forms, then he sank back on the table and exhaled. He'd found Daniel. He was so tired. He felt as if he hadn't slept forever, but he knew once he saw Daniel for himself, he would sleep. He knew the visions were gone. He didn't need them anymore.

IT WAS OVER. Carin stood back while the doctor began to stitch David's wound, and she knew she didn't have an excuse to stay any longer. Even though her eyes burned and the brightness in the room shimmered, no tears came. Maybe she was past tears. An ache of loss that had begun after the confrontation with David at the motel had intensified to the point that she knew not even tears could help ease it.

Maybe once she got away and back to her own world, it would ease. She saw David say something to Dr. Pine, then he signed the papers and sank back on the table. She knew his relief was monumental. She'd felt it when Dr. Carr had told him Daniel was alive, much the same way she had felt his frustration and pain when he'd thought his brother was dead.

She bit her bottom lip. Maybe once she wasn't close to David, once she couldn't look into his eyes, or feel his heat next to her, or inhale his scent, maybe then she could forget.

But even as she watched Dr. Carr leave the room, she knew she would never forget. Never. And she knew that she couldn't stay any longer. Without a word, she slipped out of the room and saw Dr. Carr heading down the green-tiled corridor. She went after her.

"Excuse me," she said as she neared the doctor. "Can I talk to you for just a minute?"

Dr. Carr turned to look at Carin. "What can I do for you?"

"Can you tell me exactly what the prognosis is for David's brother?"

The woman exhaled. "This morning I would have told you it wasn't good. We almost lost him. But now…" She closed her eyes for a minute, then looked back at Carin. "I'm guardedly optimistic. His lungs are functioning surprisingly well, and the infection is under control. Now his brother's here, I'm sure it's going to make a lot of difference. There's nothing worse than dealing with a patient who doesn't have anyone."

"Can David stay here to be close to his brother?"

"I'm sure that can be arranged. Dr. Pine obviously wants him here for observation. I don't think there'd be any problem with making that a seventy-two-hour period."

"Thanks. I appreciate your talking to me."

"Can I ask you something? Just who is Daniel Hart?"

"He's thirty-eight, an identical twin, and an author. He writes a popular detective series."

"What about his family?"

"There's just David and Daniel and their mother, but they aren't close to her. I think she's in Europe. David didn't know for sure."

"Where's Daniel from?"

"San Diego. He lives on a houseboat there. He was on a research trip for his next book. When he didn't come back, his brother got concerned and came looking for him."

"Are you with Mr. Hart?"

"No." She said the single word and felt as if she'd severed a lifeline. "I'm a psychologist and I was just helping David find Daniel."

"Can I ask you one more thing?"

"Sure."

"Just how *did* you find this place?"

"I didn't. David did. He had a notebook of Daniel's and he followed hunches." She didn't know why she was hedging with this woman when she knew full well how David ended up in this place. But she couldn't tell her the whole truth. That was up to David. If he ever did. "Could I see Daniel?"

The doctor shook her head. "I wish I could let you, but his visitors are restricted to immediate family. After the infection, it's not wise. But you'll be able to see him in a day or two."

"I can't stay, but would you do me a favor?"

"If I can."

"When he's able to understand, just tell him I was here, and that he was right about David."

WHEN DAVID FINALLY SAW Daniel an hour later, he walked into the intensive care cubicle and it was as if he had been there many times before. He crossed to the bed, the sound of the ventilator in the background a familiar one to him.

He went to the bed and looked down at Daniel. The image of himself, yet so different. And that difference went beyond the physical. He knew that with a certainty. And so much the same. He knew that with a certainty now, too.

Dr. Carr followed him into the space, going to the opposite side of the bed. She was talking, explaining Daniel's injuries, but David barely heard her. He stared at his brother, at the bruises that marred his jaw, the heavy taping on his ribs, the way his head had been shaved on one side to expose the skin and heavy suturing. How had she ever seen the likeness between himself and Daniel? Both of them looked like punching bags.

He touched Daniel's hand, and it was as if he was holding onto himself. "Daniel? It's me, David. I'm here. Whatever it was that brought me here, I made it."

"Mr. Hart? David?"

He looked at Dr. Carr. "Yes?"

"Don't expect too much. His head trauma was rather severe. I'm not sure how long it's going to take to get him to respond."

David looked back at Daniel. "He can hear us. He knows what's going on."

"Of course, we think comatose patients can hear, but—"

"He can hear," he said without looking away from Daniel. He'd heard her often enough over the past two days. "He knows that you were pulling for him, that you wouldn't let him leave. He heard you telling the other doctor that you wouldn't let him slip away."

"How—"

"He hears everything," David said and leaned closer to Daniel. "Someone told me that you have to believe in the unbelievable, to have faith in things that can't be touched or seen or felt." Carin had been right about so much, and he'd been so wrong.

The doctor moved and slid a chair over to David. "I guess you're going to be here for a while."

He sank down in the chair and looked at Daniel. "I'll be here for as long as it takes."

IT WAS SEVEN HOURS later when David experienced a miracle. He was almost asleep, his head against the side rail of Daniel's bed, his hand on his brother's. Without any warning, he felt Daniel move. He sat back, barely breathing, just watching his brother. Then he felt his hand move again, the pressure light but real.

He held more tightly to Daniel. Carin. If it hadn't been for her, he would have never come here. He would have been fighting the nightmares alone, having visions that terrified him.

Daniel's eyelids twitched, then slowly his eyes opened and as Dr. Carr came into the room, David heard her gasp. But David didn't look at her. "Daniel? Daniel?" he said.

He was still, his eyes oddly dilated, then he slowly looked at David, and David knew Daniel was back.

NEAR DAWN, when Daniel finally fell into a natural sleep, David walked into the corridor and leaned against the nearest wall.

"Mr. Hart?"

He turned as Dr. Carr came toward him. She'd been up all night with them. "Daniel's sleeping."

"I know. I'm going to take the tubes out when he wakes up, then you two can talk. I know you must have a lot of questions for him. I've arranged for you to have a room just down the hall. You need to get some rest."

He was exhausted, but what he needed right now was to see Carin. He needed to touch her, and hold on to her, and feel her reality. And he needed to tell her that she'd been right about everything.

"Where's Carin—Dr. Walker?"

"She left."

David stood straight. "When?"

"As soon as she knew Daniel was going to be all right, she left."

"Where did she go?" he demanded.

The doctor shook her head. "I don't know. She just said that she had to get on with things."

Lack of sleep had taken its toll, and David couldn't even think straight. "Get on with things? What things?"

"I assumed it was something professional."

I'm obsessive about a lot of things, including my work. Her voice rang in his memory. And he was obsessed with her. Hadn't he proved that her theory was valid? Maybe it hadn't been as dramatic as the airplane experience of the other set of twins, but T-11 had certainly been found by T-12. Reluctantly, but validly.

"Oh, I almost forgot. There was something she left for you." She went back to the nurse's station and returned with something in her hand. When she held it out to him, he stared at Carin's three-ring binder with Daniel's smaller book tucked inside. "She asked me to give this to you and tell you it's yours."

He stared at the book. "What?"

"She said that she didn't care what you did with it. It's all yours."

David took the binder and Daniel's research notes and held them. She'd left all of her notes, every drop of research she'd done on him. Nothing made sense at all.

"Mr. Hart, you need to rest. You're exhausted."

He was so tired he wondered if he could even walk down the hall to his room. "I know."

"It's early morning. Sleep for a few hours, then you can see Daniel again. Or call Carin." She touched his arm and urged him to go with her down the hall. "Come on. Get some sleep. Daniel's going to need you at full strength."

David went with her and when she took him into a stark hospital room with a single bed near a curtained window, he knew it would be easier to think and sort out things after he'd slept. "Thanks for getting me this room," he said. As he sank down on the edge of the bed, he looked at the doctor. "And thanks for all you've done for my brother."

"I'm just glad he's going to recover." She came closer and helped him strip off the damaged shirt. "Do you want a hospital gown?"

"No," he said and fell back on the bed, the hard mattress like a cloud of feathers to him. "Are you in any discomfort?" she asked. "Headache or anything?"

His eye throbbed, and the headache had become a constant companion. But to know he could lie down and sleep without nightmares, more than made up for all of that. "I'm fine," he murmured as he closed his eyes, the notebook resting on his chest.

"Mr. Hart?"

"Yes?"

"How did you know what I said to your brother when we almost lost him?"

He barely opened his good eye and the bright overhead light made the headache even worse. "Later."

"Fine. You sleep. I'll talk to you after you've rested."

"If Dr. Walker calls, no matter when, please tell them to let me know."

"Of course I will," she said, and as he closed his eye, he felt her take the notebook. "I'll just put this on the side table for you," she said.

As he rolled onto his side, he felt her put a light blanket over him, then he heard her cross the floor, the door opened and closed and all was silent. He exhaled and as sleep came, he sank into its deep comfort, his last thought that he wished Carin was with him. He wished that he had made things right before she left, that he'd told her he didn't care if she used him in her research, that he hadn't let her out of his sight without telling her that he loved her.

That thought sunk in so simply and sweetly that it made him smile. Love. Yes. So simple. Can't touch it, or smell it, or see it. But it was real, very real. He'd find her, as soon as Daniel could be left for a while, he'd find her. First he'd sleep, then he'd go to Carin.

When David finally woke, he felt as if he had just fallen asleep. He eased his eyes open, thankful his right eye was less swollen and he could actually see with it. But the room was dimly lit from a sidelight, and when he looked to his right at a clock on the side stand, it read eight-thirty. He glanced at the draped window and when he couldn't see any light through the slight parting where the material met, he knew it was night, not morning.

The door opened, spilling bright light from the corridor, and a nurse he'd never seen before came into the room. "Good, you're awake," she said as she came to his bedside. "Dr. Pine wanted to make sure everything was all right."

He felt stiff and sore, but the headache was gone. Before he could tell her, she pushed a thermometer in his mouth and grabbed his wrist. He lay back in the bed, staring at the ceiling until she let go of his hand and took the thermometer out of his mouth. She stared at it, then smiled. "Normal. You're normal."

I bet you think you're the last normal man in the world, Carin had said.

He knew he wasn't normal. He probably never had been, but he'd be closer once he found Carin. He pushed himself up to a sitting position, threw his legs over the side and waited for a slight faintness to recede before looking around the room.

His suitcase was by the open door to the bathroom. "How's my brother doing?"

"He's remarkable. He's out of ICU and they put him in the room across the hall. They took out the tubes and he's actually sitting up a bit."

David levered himself off the bed and stood. "I'm going to take a shower, then I'll go in to see him."

"I'll ask the doctor if that's all right."

"I'm telling you it's all right," he said, then crossed to get his bag. "Tell the doctor where I am." He looked back at the nurse by the bed. "Did I get any calls?"

"No, sir."

"Nothing at all?"

"Were you expecting something important?"

He couldn't begin to tell her how important it was for him to get to Carin. "If there's a call, will you come and get me in my brother's room?"

"Of course."

When she left, he picked up the phone and called long-distance information. After asking for the number for Carin in San Diego, he dialed but only got her answering service. "I need to talk to Dr. Walker."

"I'm sorry, sir, the doctor's out of town."

"When do you expect her back?"

"Not for at least a week, but she calls in for her messages. Did you want to leave one?"

"Tell her that David called, that Daniel's going to make it, and that David needs to see her as soon as possible."

"Do you have a number where she can contact you?"

He read the phone number off the bedside phone, then said, "And tell her David has her notes and she's going to need them for her research."

FIFTEEN MINUTES LATER, David stepped into his brother's room and found Daniel propped up in bed, the tubes all gone, and Dr. Carr helping him sip some water. When he saw David, he actually smiled.

Dr. Carr stepped back, putting the glass on the side table, and David went to the other side of the bed. "God, it's good to see you up and awake."

Daniel's voice was little more than a raspy whisper. "I can finally talk," he managed.

Dr. Carr touched Daniel on the shoulder. "I'll be back in a few minutes."

Daniel watched her leave, then looked back at David. "The doctor's pretty easy on the eyes, isn't she?"

"You're still the same," David said.

"So are you."

David knew he wasn't even close to being the person he'd been three days ago. "You're sure as hell not T. J. Pierce."

Daniel rolled his eyes upward. "If I was T. J., I'd be out of here by now and back to getting the bad guys." He looked at David. "Speaking of which, why aren't you out digging up some bones, or trying to pound facts into your students' heads?"

"I was looking for you."

"Sara told me I came in without ID, that they had no idea who I was." Daniel's voice was getting weaker and more raspy. "How'd you ever find me?"

David almost said, "I was lucky," but he stopped himself. "I found you. Leave it at that for now, and I'll explain it later."

"What's going on?"

"You're getting better."

"And you aren't going to tell me?"

David gripped the cold metal of the side rail. "I'll just say that you were right about us, about a lot of things."

Daniel frowned. "What—"

"I've got good news and bad news for you. What do you want first?"

"Good news," he said hoarsely.

David pulled his research notebook out of his pocket. "Your research. It's all there."

"I never even . . ." He looked at David as he put the notebook on the side table. "All right, the bad news?"

"Your Harley's done in. Irreparable."

David didn't know what to expect, but it was the hoarse chuckle. "Dead?"

"Close. Maybe Crazy Rick could resuscitate it."

He raised one eyebrow. "How do you know about him?"

"Let's just say we met. Leave it at that and just work on getting better. We'll worry about details later."

"Do I have a choice?" He tried to smile, but his expression was filled with weakness and David could see his strength failing.

"A choice?" Sara Carr asked as she came back into the room.

"I told him he had to work on getting better," David said.

"Good, because that's exactly what you have to do," she said, stopping by the bed to reach for Daniel's wrist. As she checked her watch, she spoke to David. "Mr. Hart, I think it's best if you let your brother rest for a while."

David touched Daniel's shoulder. "Rest and I'll be back later."

Daniel managed a weak smile before he closed his eyes and sank into the pillows that supported him. The doctor lowered Daniel's hand onto the white linen, then looked at David and motioned toward the door with her head.

David patted Daniel's shoulder. "Do what you're told," he said, then headed for the door.

Sara Carr exited after him and spoke in a low voice. "He's going to be sleeping off and on for the next forty-eight hours or so, so you might want to get some more rest for yourself."

"I can't. I need to take care of something really important." And he knew that he'd made a decision about Carin. "Do you think Daniel's stable enough for me to leave for a day or so?"

"I don't see why not. He's doing remarkably well. Just leave a number where you can be reached."

"I don't know exactly where I'll be, but I'll check in here as often as I can."

"Ask for the nurse's station up here, and if there's any problem, they'll let you know."

"Thanks."

"Can I ask where you're going to be?"

"Albuquerque, then maybe San Diego."

Chapter Fourteen

As soon as the small plane David had chartered in
Freemont landed in Albuquerque at midnight, he
found a bank of pay phones inside the terminal and
called the hospital. The nurse in charge told him that
Daniel's condition was stable. When he hung up, he
reached for the phone book and flipped it open to
residential listings for Walker. Looking at a page filled
with Walkers, he realized that he didn't know Carin's
father's or mother's name.

Then he remembered that Carin had said her sister
was a pediatrician in the city. He flipped to the Physician listings, looked under Pediatricians, and didn't
have any difficulty finding an ad for Dr. Catherine
Walker. There were two numbers, one for her office,
and one for emergencies. He didn't think twice about
dialing the emergency number.

"Dr. Walker's service. How can I help you?" a
woman asked.

"I need to get in touch with Dr. Walker as quickly
as possible."

"I need the patient's name and what the problem
is."

"This is personal."

"Sir, I suggest that you call Dr. Walker at her home directly."

"I don't have that number."

"Then call her office after nine o'clock tomorrow morning and you can speak to her then."

Frustration was building in David, but he kept his voice even. "Can you do me a favor, can you contact Dr. Walker and tell her that I need to talk to her about her sister, that it's important that I see her as quickly as possible?"

"Well, I—"

"Please, just call her. Tell her that David Hart needs to talk to her about her sister. That it's an emergency."

"All right. I'll try. I'll put you on hold and get right back to you."

The line clicked, then music came over the wire. Just when David thought the woman had forgotten about him, the music was gone and she was back on the line. "Sir?"

"Yes?"

"Dr. Walker said she'll meet you at her office in fifteen minutes."

David got the address from her, then headed out of the terminal and hailed a taxi. He gave the driver the address, then sat back, carrying Carin's book with her research notes. The cabbie drove off in a squeal of tires onto the midnight streets of Albuquerque that were almost deserted. David realized he didn't have a clue what day it even was. His life had been a blur for the past three days, and it wasn't close to stopping, not until he saw Carin.

As the taxi drove onto a downtown street lined with high rises, the cabby slowed down, then stopped in front of a structure that looked like it was all mirrors. David paid, picked up the notebook, then got out and headed for the softly lit entrance.

As he went inside the door, a security guard crossed to him. "Mr. Hart?"

"Yes."

"Go right up. Dr. Walker's on the sixth floor, suite G. She said to go inside and back to her office." He motioned to elevators behind him in the marble and brass space. "The first elevator's working and will take you to six."

"Thanks." David strode across the lobby into the elevator and pressed the button for the sixth floor.

He didn't realize just how nervous he was until the elevator began its silent ascent. If her sister didn't know where Carin was, he'd have to go back to the hospital and hope that Carin returned his calls.

The elevator came to a soft stop, the doors slid open and David stepped out into a wide hallway carpeted in soft apricot. Elegant paintings hung on neutral walls, and there wasn't a person in sight. He started to the right, passing silent suites, and finally spotted a discreet brass plaque on a door to his left. Dr. Catherine Walker, Pediatrics.

He pushed open the door and stepped into a waiting room that was a drastic departure from the understated elegance outside. In here the walls were done in cartoon murals, with deep blue carpeting, chairs were small enough for a child to use, and toys were stacked in one corner.

He crossed to the open door on the far side, looked inside and saw another door at the end of a short, wide hall. It stood open, with a light on inside. David headed toward it.

He got to the door and was stunned to see Carin there. She stood with her back to him in front of a glass-topped desk that sat in front of an expanse of windows looking onto the city at night. Her golden hair was confined in a low knot, and the tailored suit she was wearing couldn't hide her elegant curves. David felt like a tongue-tied teenager.

He'd done nothing but think about what he would say to her while he'd been on the flight, knowing it would be the most important speech of his life. But God help him, he could barely think of what to say past getting her name out. "Carin?"

At the sound of his voice, she jumped, then turned to him. David found himself facing a woman as much like Carin as a mirror image, but he knew without asking that this wasn't Carin. In that moment, so much fell into place.

"You're not Carin, are you?"

"Catherine," she said, the voice the same, yet worlds apart from Carin's. "And you must be David Hart?"

"You must be Carin's twin?"

She nodded. "Are you all right?"

He'd totally forgotten his black eye and the bandage on his temple. "It's not as bad as it looks."

"You said you had to talk to me about Carin. That it was an emergency. What's going on? Is something wrong with her?"

"Do you know where she is?"

"No, I thought you did. She was supposed to be here two days ago. If only she'd fly, it would save so much time."

David went closer to Catherine, unable to stop making comparisons with Carin. Small things were so different—the way she held her head, the way she stood. "Why won't she fly?" he asked, and knew before the answer came.

"I was on a plane a few years ago and there were problems. Carin wasn't anywhere around, yet she experienced it herself. She had a premonition, and when the plane almost crashed, she experienced it as if she'd been there." Catherine shook her head. "I don't expect you to understand, but twins have something that other brothers or sisters don't have."

"I understand," he said.

"Most people don't. My sister didn't, but she wouldn't let it go. You must know she's a psychologist, but she's never practiced. She's used her own money to fund a study into the bonding of twins, into links that go beyond the five senses."

"Her own money?"

"Her trust fund from our grandfather."

She was independently wealthy, too. The woman was one surprise after the other. "She's determined, isn't she?"

"She has her obsessions," Catherine said with a small smile. "But she's brilliant. What I don't understand is why you called, and why you got me here, and why you said there was an emergency with Carin."

"I'd like to hear his answers for that too, Cathy," someone said from behind David.

He turned and saw Carin in the doorway to the office, her hair windblown from the convertible, her white shorts and pale blue tank top mussed from the long drive. And when her navy blue eyes met his, he knew he'd never seen anyone more beautiful in his life. And at that moment, his whole life came into sharp focus.

"Carrie," Catherine said and hurried around David to her sister. She hugged her, then moved back, her hands still on her shoulders. "Are you going to explain what's going on? I thought you'd dropped off the face of the earth. You were supposed to be here days ago."

Carin touched her sister's cheek. "I ran into some problems, but I made it. Your housekeeper said you were in here." She looked past Catherine at David. "How's Daniel?"

"He's going to make it."

She looked relieved. He knew that she genuinely cared about Daniel. Then she looked at the binder he was still holding. "Why are you here?"

He held out her book. "You forgot this."

"I gave it to you." She drew back and hugged her arms around herself, but didn't take her eyes off David. "Didn't the doctor tell you?"

"She told me, but it's yours. It's not mine. It's your study. It's your money that's in it."

"But you—"

"I came here to find you to tell you you were right about everything." He couldn't take his eyes off her. "And I was wrong. I was completely wrong."

"Excuse me," Catherine said. "What's going on here?"

Carin never looked away from David. "Cathy, can I use your office for a while? I'll come by your house in an hour or so. I . . . I need to straighten things out with Mr. Hart."

"I guess so. I'll get going and we can talk when you get to the house."

"Thanks."

Catherine crossed to her desk, then went back to Carin by the door. "Don't keep me waiting all night," she said to Carin, then turned to David. "Nice meeting you, Mr. Hart," she said, then went out, closing the door behind her.

The silence in the room was deafening. David wanted to go to Carin, to touch her, but he didn't. He waited, watching her. God, how could he have ever let her go? Then he had the chilling thought that it might be too late.

He still had her book, and he held it out to her. "I meant it, this is yours. And I'll do whatever you want to validate your study. Everything you tried to tell me was true. I actually experienced what Daniel was going through. I don't know if he was doing it, or if it was me, or if it was both of us. But without you, I don't think I would have gone after him."

She didn't come closer or take the book. "And you wouldn't have met Willy, or Crazy Rick, or Trig, or almost gotten killed at The Pit."

And he wouldn't have fallen in love with her. "I wouldn't change any of that."

"Are you serious?" she asked as she let her purse slip onto a chair.

"Absolutely."

"Your eye?"

"I can see."

"Your cut?"

"It's nothing. Just six stitches. Don't you want your notes back?"

"I can't use them."

He frowned at her, hating the distance between them. "What are you talking about?"

Finally she came toward him, and he caught the sweetness of fresh air and flowers that seemed to cling to Carin. "I can't use them because I'm not objective anymore."

She stopped right in front of him, leaving barely a foot of space as a buffer between them. "Carin, if I've ruined things for you, I'm sorry. I never meant to. It's just...these past few days have been..." He couldn't think of any word that could describe what he'd gone through.

"Confusing?" she asked.

"Yes."

She came closer and took the book from him. "Frustrating?"

"Yes."

She was so close he could literally feel her body heat through the thin cotton of his shirt. She tossed the notebook onto the desk, then unexpectedly touched the bandage at his temple. "Painful?"

"Sometimes."

Her finger trailed to his tender eye. "Dangerous?"

He could feel his response to her come suddenly and dramatically. "Absolutely," he whispered. "Why didn't you tell me you were a twin?"

Her finger slowly traced the line of his cheek, and he could feel the unsteadiness in her touch. "I didn't think about it until it was too late. You let me know what you thought, how you thought, and I didn't think it would make any difference.'' Her hand stilled on him. ''Why are you here?'' she breathed.

''I had to find you.''

''Why?''

He felt her touch on him, and looked into her eyes. For a heartbeat he felt real fear. What if he told her he loved her, and she walked away? Then she came even closer, her body barely touching his, and she smiled up at him. ''Because I love you,'' he whispered.

''Are you sure?''

He let himself reach out to her, and the moment he felt her softness under his hands, he knew there was no turning back. ''Don't analyze this, Doctor, just tell me that it's not too late.''

She reached out, quickly touching her lips to his, then she drew back and her smile was brilliant. ''You didn't ask why I'm not objective enough to do the study.''

The last thing he wanted to talk about was the damned study, but he murmured, ''Why?''

''Because I've become emotionally involved with one of my subjects. T-12. You might know him by the name of David Hart.''

He smiled and drew her to him. He buried his face in the fragrance of her hair, held onto her and breathed, ''How emotionally involved?''

''I love him,'' she said. ''And loving someone takes away your objectivity.''

David felt his heart settle, and when Carin began to work her hands under his shirt, he felt his breath catch. "Do you want to do a study on that loss of objectivity?"

She drew back just enough to look up into his face. "A study? That has possibilities." Slowly she began to unbutton his shirt. "Great possibilities." She tugged his shirt free of his slacks. "What do you think?"

As her hands spread warmly on his chest, he found his ability to talk hampered just a bit. "I like your ideas, but here?"

She moved away from him, went to the door, flipped the lock, then turned off the glaring overhead light. The lights from the city filtered into the room, giving it an almost ethereal tone. Carin came back to David. "My sister won't mind. What do *you* think?"

He framed her face with his hands and looked with wonder into her eyes. "Let's get started."

Epilogue

Dreams.

For two weeks David hadn't dreamed. He had fallen into sleep, into peace and quiet, and no dreams.

No nightmares, no visions, just peace.

Until now.

The dream came to him on silent cat's feet, there before he knew it, with a life of its own.

Carin. She was near him, looking at him, her deep blue eyes veiled and her hands reaching out to him. A swirl of soft whiteness was around her and he needed her with an intensity that knew no bounds. He wanted to touch her, to hold her and never let her go, but he couldn't move.

With agonizing slowness, she came toward him, and when she finally touched him, when he finally felt her hand on his skin, he thought he would explode with need.

A smile touched her lips as her hands moved over him, skimming over his chest, trailing to his waist, then lower, and when he would have cried out, her lips covered his. Taste, heat, need, all mingled, and when

Carin moved back, when her lips left his, when her touch was gone, David cried out.

"David, David," Carin murmured softly, and the dream fled.

David woke in shadows, his breathing ragged and his desire for Carin a real thing. And she was there. He felt her heat against his heat, her skin against his, her breasts pressed to his chest. He buried his face in her hair and held her tightly, letting the sensation of her saturate his mind and body. Every curve, every gentle swelling of her. He had to force himself to take a breath.

"David, what's wrong?" she whispered through the darkness as the houseboat rose and fell gently on the water.

He closed his eyes tightly as he laced his fingers in the silky veil of her hair. "Nothing, nothing," he murmured.

"You weren't having the dreams again, were you?"

"Dreams," he echoed.

She moved back slightly, and he opened his eyes as she raised herself on one elbow to look down at him. Her other hand rested on his stomach, and her hair fell in a silky veil around her shoulders. He could see the worry on her face. "Is it Daniel?"

"No." He reached out to touch with the tips of his fingers the heat of her naked shoulder, then trailed them up the sweep of her throat to her chin. He felt her tremble at his touch, and the dream faded even more. "He's fine. I called while you were asleep. He'll be released in a week."

She kissed him quickly and fiercely, then drew back before he could really taste her. "That's a relief. I thought the dreams were back."

"It was a dream, but not about Daniel." He slipped his hand under the veil of her hair, to the heat of her neck. "It was about you."

"What about me?"

"You were with me, but I knew you were leaving."

She laughed softly, but the sound was unsteady. "That *was* a dream." She pressed a kiss to his chest, then drew back. "Trivia question."

"Carin, I don't want to guess what movie had the line, 'Make my day,' in it."

"No movies. A simple question. All right?"

He could barely think of anything but her, and how badly he wanted her, and how he would never get enough of her. "Go ahead."

"Answer me this. What is reality?"

He exhaled. "I don't—"

"Humor me," she said as she traced his nipple with the tip of her finger. "Tell me what reality is."

He looked at her. "*You* are reality."

"Good. But I can go one better on that. This, where we are right now, this is reality. Reality is us getting married in the hospital with Daniel, your best man, propped up in bed, and Sara standing up for me." Her hand skimmed to his waist. "Reality is having our first night as a married couple at the No-Tell Motel, in our favorite room, and letting you take me back to Shadow Canyon to scrape our initials in the wall. Reality is you buying a house near the university so I can have a part of it for my work."

Her hand moved lower. "Reality is me loving you so much that you'll never be able to get rid of me."

"I'll never try to get rid of you." His voice grew hoarse with desire as she touched him just as she had in the dream. "Never."

"Well, I wouldn't go quietly, Mr. Hart," she breathed as she moved until she was over him, her hands pressed to the pillow on either side of his head. Then she slowly lowered herself on him until he fit deep inside her as if they'd both been created just for this moment. "Or I'd get Trig to convince you that you really need me," she said as she began to move.

He inhaled on a shudder as sensations began to rock him. He wanted to tell her that she was way past fine, that she redefined the meaning of perfection, but as the pleasure grew and expanded into an exquisite joy, it went beyond words. And he met reality face-to-face.

Reality was Carin with him. Carin, his obsession.

**American Romance invites you to celebrate
a decade of success....**

It's a year of celebration for American Romance, as we commemorate a milestone achievement—10 years of bringing you the kinds of romance novels you want to read, by the authors you've come to love.

And we're not stopping now! In the months ahead, we'll be bringing you more of the adventures of a lifetime...and some superspecial anniversary surprises.

We've got lots in store, so mark your calendars to join us, beginning in August, for all the fun of our 10th Anniversary year....

AMERICAN ROMANCE
We'll rouse your lust for adventure!

HARLEQUIN®

AMERICAN ◆ ROMANCE®

**Four new stars shine a silvery light on
American Romance's 10th Anniversary!**

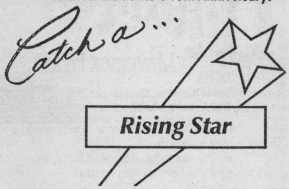

Catch a...

Rising Star

Over the past decade, American Romance has launched
over 40 first-time authors—and made stars of a dozen
more. And in August a new constellation appears—
the stars of tomorrow—four authors brand-new to
American Romance:

#497 **AT HER CAPTAIN'S COMMAND**
      by Patricia Chandler
#498 **DATE WITH AN OUTLAW** by Lynn Lockhart
#499 **ONE FOOT IN HEAVEN** by Laraine McDaniel
#500 **WILD CARD WEDDING** by Jule McBride

In August 1993 catch the excitement—
Catch a "Rising Star"!   HARSTAR